FANNY CROSBY SPEAKS AGAIN

120 hymns by

Fanny Jane Crosby

never before published

Edited by Donald P. Hustad

HOPE PUBLISHING COMPANY
CAROL STREAM, ILLINOIS 60187

Foreword

Contemporary hymnologists might disagree sharply about the significance of the literary work of Fanny Jane Crosby (1820–1915). Nevertheless, it is little short of amazing that her most definitive biography has been written by a thirty-year-old Lutheran clergyman and published within the last year, six decades after her death. (Bernard Ruffin, *Fanny Crosby*, United Church Press, 1976). Reading it, one can have little doubt that this was a remarkable woman who had a profound influence on the American church scene during the last one-third of the nineteenth century and on into the twentieth.

Though she lived to be ninety-five years of age, most of Fanny Crosby's best hymns were written in a twenty-five year span, from 1864 to 1889. To be sure, she had already achieved considerable reputation as a poet (as well as a fine singer, organist and harpist) in her earlier years as a student and later as a teacher, at the New York City Institution for the Blind. Here she had met and performed for four of our country's presidents—John Tyler, John Quincy Adams, Andrew Johnson and Grover Cleveland—as well as William Henry Seward (Lincoln's Secretary of State), William Cullen Bryant, Stephen A. Douglas and Jefferson Davis. In 1844, at the age of 24, she had published *The Blind Girl and Other Poems*, which had a fair sale. She had also enjoyed some success writing secular song lyrics (including "minstrels") for composer George Frederick Root.

It seems indisputable that Fanny Crosby turned to hymn-writing as the result of a profound religious experience in 1850. The evangelical revival had been running for several months in the Broadway Tabernacle (Methodist) on 30th Street in New York City. For some time, Fanny had been in a state of depression, brought on by the conviction that she was not truly a Christian. She evidently attended the Tabernacle nightly for several weeks, and had "gone forward to the altar" twice without receiving peace. Finally, on November 20, 1850, during the singing of Isaac Watts' "Alas, and did my Savior bleed," she found release and assurance. As she said: "My very soul was flooded with celestial light. . . . For the first time I realized that I had been trying to hold the world in one hand and the Lord in the other."

It was yet another fourteen years before Fanny Crosby turned her talent to the writing of hymns. It all began on February 2, 1864 when she met William B. Bradbury, famed associate of Lowell Mason and the writer of public school music and the new Sunday School hymns. Bradbury gave her an assignment to write both a sacred and a secular (Civil War) song, and she passed the test with flying colors. Accordingly, she went to work for William B. Bradbury and Company, and the illustrious composer said, "While I have a publishing company, you will always have work."

Four years later, on January 7, 1868, Bradbury died at the age of fifty-one. His publishing operation was taken over by Sylvester Main, who had known Fanny Crosby as a young girl, and Lucius Horatio Biglow, and they formed the Biglow and Main Company, which eventually became the largest publisher of gospel music in the country. Mrs. Crosby—as she was usually called, though she was married to Alexander Van Alstyne, a blind musician—was affiliated with Biglow and Main for the rest of her life.

During her most productive years, Fanny Crosby produced at least three or four hymns a week, and, according to her own records, wrote a total of 5959 poems for Biglow and Main. Evidently they never had a written or an exclusive contract, for she also supplied many texts for William J. Kirkpatrick and John R. Sweney, who published with the John J. Hood Company in Philadelphia, and for other composers and publishers. Even so, up to one-half of each Biglow and Main collection was based on her lyrics, released under several versions of her own name and more than two hundred pseudonyms. It has been variously estimated that she wrote somewhere between six and nine thousand texts in her lifetime. At least three thousand were published, set to music by a long list of composers, including William Howard Doane, Robert Lowry, Ira D. Sankey, William J. Kirkpatrick, John R. Sweney, William F. Sherwin, Phoebe Palmer Knapp, George C. Stebbins, Charles H. Gabriel, I. Allan Sankey, and Hubert P. Main, son of Sylvester Main, who edited many of the Biglow and Main publications.

Most of the poems were created during the night hours, when other folk were asleep. Fanny never wrote them down—actually, she was not very proficient in the use of Braille. After a period of prayer and meditation, she just composed the verses in her mind, memorized them and dictated them to a friend or a secretary, after waking the next morning. It is said that, on one occasion, she "stored up" as many as forty poems in her mind, before having them transcribed. Obviously, she had a phenomenal memory!

What is even more amazing is that many of the lyrics were written to previously composed music which she had also memorized after one or two hearings. These were undoubtedly the first to be published, because the composers were usually editors and compilers of songbooks, and they benefited most financially from their sale.

The standard fee paid the author of a hymn-poem in the mid-nineteenth century was $2.00 per song. As a result, Fanny Crosby's income from writing never exceeded $500 annually. In later years, the standard rate may have gone as high as $10, but hers remained the same, and many of her friends protested that she was being cheated. But Fanny seemed to be "committed to poverty," giving much of her meager income to less fortunate persons, to whom she constantly ministered, both physically and spiritually. In later life, Biglow and Main gave her $8.00 a week whether she produced poems or not, and Ira D. Sankey (who became president of the company in 1895) paid the rent on her living quarters in Bridgeport, Connecticut, beginning in 1900. There was some additional income from the sale of an autobiography and another book of verse, but at her death her total estate was valued at only $2,000!

The poems which remained in the files of Biglow and Main at Fanny Crosby's death were probably those she had written "on her own." These manuscripts came into the possession of Hope Publishing Company when they purchased the Biglow and Main Company in 1922, and have remained in their safekeeping ever since. Obviously, since Fanny Crosby never learned to write more than her own name, they are not in her handwriting. In the 1870's, she often dropped in at the Biglow and Main offices near her residence on East Ninth Street in New York City, to dictate her poems; no doubt, on occasion, a friend or a company secretary stopped by her apartment to write them down. In the late 1890's she lived in Brooklyn near her close friends, the Ira D. Sankeys and the George C. Stebbinss, and they frequently got together. After 1900, when she moved to Bridgeport, Connecticut, the hymns were no doubt recorded by Carolyn Ryder, her companion, or Eva G. Cleaveland, a professional secretary who was engaged to handle her heavy load of counseling correspondence during the last years.

From more than one thousand unpublished poems, we have chosen to print one hundred twenty. Many of these texts were left without any punctuation, just as they had been written down from dictation on a typical morning in Fanny Crosby's life. We have included all the essential information left on the manuscript page—sometimes the date or the place of writing, and frequently a folio number which indicated the sequence of her contributions to Biglow and Main. (Note that no. 889 is dated January 10, 1878, and no. 5384, February 11, 1903.) This number is usually inscribed at the upper left of the page, often with a large, scrawled "E" written in ink—of unknown significance. (See the photograph elsewhere in this volume.) Note that the chronicler lost track of the sequence after no. 3243 (March 23, 1892) and regained it with no. 3635 (October 27, 1893).

In a few instances, phrases are obviously wrong or are incomplete—mistakes that we must blame on the *amanuensis*, not on Fanny herself. If words have been added for this publication, they are enclosed in brackets [ ]; if they have been changed, they are in parentheses ( ). Otherwise, with the exception of adding punctuation and correcting the spelling, the verses remain as we found them.

So far as we know, none of these poems of Fanny Crosby have been published before. They appear in this collection in chronological order, as best as we can determine it; a few that are undated and unnumbered are placed in the back. The number of "transcribers" who assisted the blind poetess could be determined by a handwriting expert; it can also be guessed from the similarity and the variety of page style, including the form and placement of the name and date. The typical sheet is about 8" x 11" or 8" x 14", but there are many variations in the size and the quality of the paper used.

It was most intriguing to discover that thirty-four of the manuscripts carry the impression of one of five different "embossing seals." Our guess is that each of these was used by an individual at the Biglow and Main Company in a manner similar to a notary public seal or a personal rubber stamp. The most frequently used imprint has the outline of the capitol building with its dome and two wings, and above, the single word "CONGRESS." It first appeared on a sheet dated 1872 and was used almost exclusively through 1885, once in 1891 and once in 1896. Another seal carried the name "NOLIA MILLS" in the middle of a small wreath, and was used once in 1875 and twice in 1876.

Three different seals consist of a simple word or phrase. "FA-VORITE" appeared once in 1887 and once in 1892. "HAMIL-TON" was used on twelve manuscripts between 1890 and 1899. "ISLAND CITY"—probably for Manhattan Island—was used only once, in 1892. We have no way of determining who used the seals and what they signified. We might guess that "CON-GRESS" may have been the seal of Hubert P. Main, who worked closely with Fanny Crosby in the early days. "HAMILTON" might possibly have been used by I. Allan Sankey, son of the evangelistic singer, whose handwriting appears on a number of pages dated after 1890.

It is difficult to predict whether or not these verses have any potential for use in contemporary worship or revivalism. They were probably not considered to be Fanny Crosby's best work, otherwise some musician would have already set them to music. The language often seems excessively flowery and dated, and in many instances the syntax is awkward, even by nineteenth century standards. At the same time, these 120 poems show considerable diversity of subject and style. Some are quite strong objective hymns of praise. Furthermore, there is considerable variety of meter, rhyme and rhythm. Fanny never tried to influence the composers or the publishers to choose one poem rather than another. As she said (in *Fanny Crosby's Life Story*, published in 1905):

> I made no pretense of being able to do this selecting myself—it was always performed by others; and I often find myself wondering whether some hymn may not have been suppressed, that was of real merit, while others less worthy, were put to the fore. One cannot always determine at first sight, concerning products of the pen, which will most forcibly strike the public mind and heart.

Perhaps few people today would argue that Fanny Crosby was a truly great poet. She herself had a modest view of her own talent and considered that Frances Ridley Havergal, her friend and contemporary in England, wrote better hymns than she. But she obviously ministered and communicated to the nineteenth century American mind and culture, which someone has called "the most sentimental the world has even known." Most of her songs were experience-oriented and they still form a strong core of the subjective hymnody used in our churches; for instance, the *Methodist Hymnal*, 1964 includes nine of her texts and the *Baptist Hymnal*, 1975 has twelve. There is probably little to be gained in debating the strength or weakness of hymns that have already endured and sustained Christian faith for one hundred years, and are still being sung!

Students of hymnology may find some interest in the notes we have added to many of the poems; others may choose to ignore them completely. Should any serious researcher care to examine the manuscripts personally, they may be seen in the offices of Hope Publishing Company in Carol Stream, Illinois.

We do recommend that you read the poems through, to share something of the heart of this woman who must have been a spiritual giant, though physically she was only four feet, nine inches tall. You may echo the reaction of Margaret Clarkson, a poet and hymn writer of today, who recently examined our typed copies of these manuscripts.

> Thank you for giving me the beautiful experience of an hour with Fanny J. Crosby!... When my hour or so was finished, I felt richly blessed. I had been in the presence of a great spirit, a saint of God. The things for which she praised God, I too praise Him. The struggles she knew, I know today. The glory of the Heavenly Home that blessed her way still beckons me on and blesses mine. I wonder if anyone reading my works a hundred years from now will ever so identify me with God's pilgrims as her works identify her?

> And to think that with all that colorful, descriptive language, she had never seen what she so vividly described of earth's beauties. How wonderful must have been the eyes of her heart! Perhaps this is not so surprising. I think she looked on the face of God.

The management of Hope Publishing Company feels that it would be pointless, and even improper, to seek financial gain from these previously-unpublished poems. In 1977, all Christians are the rightful heirs of Fanny Crosby's legacy in her life and her work. For this reason, they are free to be used in any way. We ask only that if they are printed, with or without music, that the page carry this notice: Words © Copyright, 1977, by Hope Publishing Company. Used by permission.

The company has also requested that all of the royalties from the sale of this book be assigned to the Fanny Crosby Memorial Home in Bridgeport, Connecticut. It was established in 1924 as a Home for the Aged in memory of the blind poet hymn writer who spent her final years as a resident of that city.

We offer this little volume in memory of Fanny Jane Crosby. She was probably one of the most selfless people who has ever lived, and deserves the title Bernard Ruffin gives her—"The Protestant Saint."

February 1, 1977   Donald P. Hustad, Editor
                                                   Hope Publishing Company

Fanny Crosby at 25

Fanny Crosby at 78

Fanny Crosby at 92

Our Bright Home Above.

Words by FANNY CROSBY.   *Music by* WM. B. BRADBURY.

1. We are going, we are going, To a home beyond the skies, Where the fields are robed in beauty, And the sunlight never dies

D.C. We are going, we are going, To a home beyond the skies, Where the fields are robed in beauty, And the sunlight never dies

Where the fount of joy is flowing In the valley green and fair, We shall dwell in love together, There will be no parting there

2. We are going, we are going,
   And the music we have heard
Like the echo of the woodland,
   Or the carol of a bird;
With the rosy light of morning
   On the calm and fragrant air,
Still it murmurs, softly murmurs,
   There will be no parting there.
         We are going, &c.

3. We are going, we are going,
   Where the day of life is o'er—
To that pure and happy region
   Where our friends have gone before;
They are singing with the angels
   In that land so bright and fair;
We shall dwell with them forever,
   There will be no parting there.
         We are going, &c.

Reproduction of the first hymn written by Fanny Crosby in 1864. This appeared in the *Golden Censer,* edited by William B. Bradbury and published by Biglow & Main, New York.

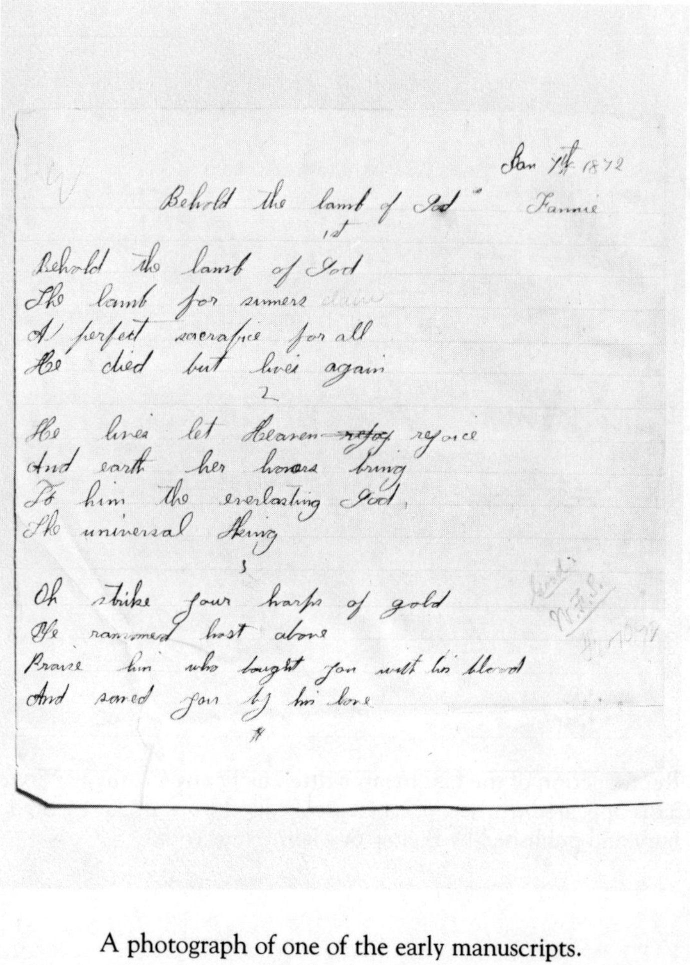

A photograph of one of the early manuscripts.

A photograph of hymn #2582 showing the "Hamilton" embossing seal. Dated March 17, 1893, it is entitled "Gather the Children."

My dear Hugh:

I received this letter which I will mail you, knowing you are the one to answer it. In answer to yours of today, you did write of Miss Holden coming and I thank you. We wrote her and she will be here tomorrow.

Well how are you? I must confess I was surprised to hear you had moved and I am quite anxious to see your new place. I have no doubt you have done wisely.

Now take good care of yourself this winter. If you only knew how much I think of you all, and of you personally. You would be sure that I love you just as well as ever and a good deal more so. Give my love to the president, my girl and everybody connected with the establishment. The Lord bless the firm of Biglow and Main is the earnest wish of your friend.

Fanny J. Crosby

January 27, 1908
226 Webb St.
Bridgeport, Ct.

Ed.   This is a letter to Hubert P. Main, the principal editor and compiler of hymnbooks at the Biglow & Main Company in New York City. In her work for the company, Fanny Crosby was closely associated with him for almost fifty years.

Each Christmas, it was Fanny's practice to send a verse to her friends at the "store" (Biglow and Main). Only one such greeting still survives and, although undated, it was probably written around the turn of the century. The "honored president" in the poem refers, no doubt, to Ira D. Sankey and "brother Hugh" to Hubert P. Main. "Louie Glatz and dear Miss Dyer" must have been faithful employees and the use of the word "patrons" in the Victorian sense is totally consistent with her understanding of her relationship with her publisher.

> Honored president, I hail thee,
>   And my loyal brother Hugh,
> Round my heart you both are clinging,
>   With affection firm and true.
> Louie Glatz and dear Miss Dyer,
>   Happy greetings one and all,
> While I sing my yearly carol,
>   And your treasured names recall.
>
> Lo, again a mighty chorus,
>   Wakes the earth and fills the sky,
> Peace, good will to every nation,
>   Glory be to God on high.
> And we look, by faith directed,
>   To the pure transcendent morn,
> When in Bethlehem of Juda
>   Our Redeemer Christ was born.
>
> Merry Christmas, Merry Christmas,
>   All my friends and patrons dear!
> May our Father's richest blessing
>   Rest upon the coming year;
> And at last beyond the river
>   May we join the ransomed throng,
> In the bright, the bright forever,
>   In the summer land of song.

> Affectionately dedicated to my friends at the Store
>   With love
>   Fanny J. Crosby

Awake, awake! let every heart
    In loudest praise adore
The great eternal Lord of all,
    Who reigns forever more.
He paints the orient sky of morn,
    He gives the flower its hue,
And gently o'er its fragrant leaves
    He drops the pearly dew.

Chorus: Strangers, pilgrims here below,
        He will lead us while we go;
        Where the cooling waters flow,
        His hand our steps will guide.

Awake, exalt His glorious name;
    And on this holy day,
Rejoicing in the house of prayer,
    Your grateful homage pay.
As o'er the earth the genial sun
    A radiant luster throws,
So in the bosom where He dwells
    The light of mercy glows.
                        Chorus.

How sweet when youthful voices join
    To sing His pard'ning love,
While angels waft the joyful strain
    To purer worlds above.
Awake, awake! let every heart
    In loudest praise adore
The great eternal Lord of all,
    Who reigns forever more.
                        Chorus.

                    F.J.C.   1867

The manuscript has the penciled word "good" at the top. The text appears to be in a brown ink, while the initials and number at the bottom are in red ink in another handwriting. If "1867" is a date, this may be the oldest of the manuscripts; Fanny Crosby wrote her first hymn for William B. Bradbury in 1864.

2

Never Turn Back

Fannie Crosby

Never turn back when the soul has enlisted
Under the banner of Jesus our King.
Stand by your colors, determined to conquer;
Stand by your colors, rejoice while you sing.

Chorus: Marching to glory, we are marching to glory,
Bright is the day-beam that shines on our way;
Marching to glory, we are marching to glory,
This be our watch-word forever and aye.

Never turn back though the world may recall you,
Tempting the heart from its duty aside;
Look to your armor, be ready for battle!
Follow the steps of your Savior and guide.
Chorus.

Never turn back when the foe is advancing,
Hurling the arrows of death on your track.
Meet him with boldness, the Lord will defend you;
Lose not your courage, O, never turn back.
Chorus.

What is the peril or strife of a moment?
What are the struggles and {toils} of a day?
What, to the (crowns) and the joy of the victor,
Fadeless, immortal, that pass not away.
Chorus.

Sep. 20th, 1871

Ed. This and the following poem were on opposite sides of a ledger sheet, probably transcribed by one of Fanny Crosby's underprivileged friends or neighbors. The penmanship was poor and there were many misspellings.

In the fourth stanza, third line, the word "crowns" appeared as "crowned." At the bottom are the notations "Royal Diadem"—a song book title—and "W.F.S." (for William F. Sherwin.)

No Friend like Jesus

Fannie Crosby

1st
No friend is like the savior
No love like his so true
It comes to us in blessings
That fall like balmly dew
With each return of morning
His tender care we see
His arm is still around us
Where ever we may be

Cho.   No friend is like the savior
No love like his so true
It comes to us in blessings
That fall like balmy dew

2nd
Yet more than earthly comfort
His gracious hand bestows
From him a blessed fountian
Of liveing water flows
To every one that thirseth
That water he will give
For he has said come hither
Oh drink and ye shall live
Cho.

3d
Thou art the way Oh savior
And thou the truth devine
The joy of life eternal
And life itselfe is thine
Thou art the rock of ages
The souls abideing rest
The God of our salvation
In thee we all are blest.
Cho.

Sep 20th 1871.

Ed.   This page appears exactly at it was written down, without corrections. See previous editorial note.

4

Fannie

Sabbath Bells

Sweetly chime the sabbath bells—
  Come, come away;
Loud and clear their music swells—
  Come, come away.
Friends and teachers all to meet,
  Joyful in the dear retreat,
Where the good and faithful meet—
  Come, come away.

Though the winter winds may blow—
  Come, come away;
Never heed the falling snow—
  Come, come away.
Gather in the house of prayer,
  All is bright and cheerful there;
Now its dear delight to share—
  Come, come away.

Hear the sabbath bells again—
  Come, come away;
Still they ring in tuneful strain—
  Come, come away.
Hark! their gentle echoes say:
  "Come to Jesus, learn to pray."
Children, you may come today—
  Come, come away.

Ed.   This Sunday school poem is written with fine Spencerian penmanship, in ink that now
appears purple. Some editor has divided the stanzas by wavy, red pen-lines and written
"1872" in the upper right corner. This is presumed to be a date.

A Child of Jesus

1872

A child of Jesus! O how sweet
  These precious words to hear;
No music breathed by mortal tongue
  Was ever half so dear.
A child of Jesus! blissful hope
  That fills me day by day
With joy the world can never give,
  And never take away.

A child of Jesus! near the cross
  My soul would still abide,
And feel, beneath His watchful care,
  Its every want supplied.
A child of Jesus, happy thought!
  Be this forever mine,
To see, through every gathering cloud,
  My Father's glory shine.

A child of Jesus, owned, and blessed
  By Him who died for me;
His wondrous love, His pard'ning grace,
  My song in heaven shall be;
A child of Jesus! O how sweet
  These precious words to hear;
No music breathed by mortal tongue
  Was ever half so dear.

Fanny J. Crosby

Ed.   The number 1872 (presumably a date) and the name at the bottom are in red ink, while the poem itself is in black. The embossed seal "CONGRESS" is at the upper right.

6

Jan. 7th, 1872
Fannie

Behold the Lamb of God

Behold the Lamb of God,
  The lamb for sinners slain;
A perfect sacrifice for all,
  He died, but lives again.

He lives—let Heaven rejoice!
  And earth her honors bring
To Him, the everlasting God,
  The universal King.

Oh, strike your harps of gold,
  Ye ransomed host above.
Praise Him who bought you with His blood,
  And saved you by His love.

Ed.   The word "slain" at the end of line two was omitted in the original and penciled in later. The 8″ x 8″ sheet was cut from a larger piece of ruled paper and carries the embossed seal "CONGRESS." In the margin is the notation in pencil: "Good. W.F.S. Feb. 10/72"—evidently written by William F. Sherwin.

Pray On

By *Fannie J. Crosby*
Sept. 25, 1874

Pray on, never doubting, the answer will come,
  The blessing will surely descend;
The words of our Savior are "Yea" and "Amen";
  Believe and pray on to the end.

Chorus: Pray on, never doubting, cling fast to the rock,
  Whose shadow our souls will defend;
  Abiding in hope and the strength of the Lord,
  Believe and pray on to the end.

Pray on, never fearing, the cloud may be dark,
  But mercy is smiling above;
The mist will be cleared, and our vision behold
  The sunlight of infinite love.
        Chorus.

Pray on, never fainting, the morning will break,
  The dew of God's grace will descend;
Tho' tried in the furnace, oh, be not dismayed;
  Endure, and pray on to the end.
        Chorus.

Pray on without ceasing, oh, pray at the door,
  And Jesus will open at last;
Believing, enduring, and trusting in God,
  Pray on till our life work is past.
        Chorus.

Ed. On the back of this manuscript, another hand has penciled a completely different
  stanza:
    Shout with the legions of angels,
      Waking the earth and sky,
    "Glory to God on high!"
      Jesus, the hope of His people,
    Jesus our Savior is born;
      Welcome His birthday morn.

8

When thy cup is mixed with sorrow—
Look beyond, look beyond!
There will come a bright tomorrow—
Look beyond, look beyond!
O'er the darkest clouds of night
Hope still hangs her beacon light;
Through the glass that faith doth lend,
Ever trusting, look beyond!

When for higher pleasure pining—
Look beyond, look beyond!
In thy Savior's arms reclining—
Look beyond, look beyond!
Only He can know thy fears,
Soothe thy heart and dry thy tears;
He, thy best and truest friend,
Bids thee, trusting, look beyond!

Though thy dearest ties may sever—
Look beyond, look beyond!
Parted here but not forever—
Look beyond, look beyond!
From their bright celestial dome
Heavenly voices call thee home,
While thy Brother and thy Friend
Bids thee, trusting, look beyond!

Fannie Crosby

Ed.   This copy has a distinctly "amateur" quality in appearance and spelling, and was
probably penned by one of Fanny's neighbors.

Little Hands

By *Fannie J. Crosby*   July 17th, 1875

Little hands were made to labor,
  Little hearts to love and pray,
Little feet to follow Jesus
  In the straight and narrow way.
Hands and heart and feet together
  In their duties must agree,
Cheerful workers, ever toiling,
  Like the busy bee.

Little tongues were made to scatter
  Loving words like music sweet,
Little minds, to keep as treasures
  What they learn at Jesus' feet;
Little tongues and minds together
  In their duty must agree,
Cheerful workers, ever toiling,
  Like the busy bee.

Little eyes were made to sparkle,
  Making all around them bright;
Little souls to live for Jesus,
  Walking in His blessed light;
Little eyes and souls together
  In their duties must agree,
Cheerful workers, ever toiling,
  Like the busy bee.

Jesus tells us we must love Him
  With our heart and soul and mind,
Pleasant work for little children,
  If we ask Him, we shall find.
May our hands be always willing
  And our hearts in love agree,
Cheerful workers, ever toiling,
  Like the busy bee.

Ed.   "NOLIA MILLS" appears embossed at upper left. There is also a "Biglow & Main"
rubber stamp at upper right with the same date as the one written. In the third stanza,
third line, the first word "little" was inserted after completion.

10

Fanny Crosby   Feby. 17/76

His eye is over all His works,
   He slumbers not, nor sleeps;
But 'neath the shadow of His wings
   His faithful ones He keeps.

Chorus: Then shout aloud and sing,
          The Lord Himself is King!
          Let all the earth rejoice with mirth,
          And lasting honors bring.

The countless orbs that gem the sky
   Are guided by His hand,
The mighty billows of the sea
   Roll on at His command.
                 Chorus.

The seasons at His bidding come
   With joy and beauty (crowned);
They bring the sweet refreshing flowers,
   And scatter fruit around.
                 Chorus.

He numbers every grain of sand
   Upon the wave-girt shore;
Great is the Lord, the Lord of hosts,
   O praise Him evermore!
                 Chorus.

Ed.   Stanza three, line two, ends with the word "crown" in the original. The "CONGRESS"
seal is embossed at upper right.

11

Fanny Crosby   Feby. 25th, 1876

A life beyond—O thought sublime—
    Beyond the checkered scenes of time,
Where they who sow and they who reap
    Shall wake in bliss, no more to weep.
A life beyond, whose joy untold
    The poor in spirit shall behold;
The (pure) in heart their God shall see,
    And near His glorious throne shall be.

A world beyond—no mortal eye
    Has looked upon its radiant sky;
No mortal ear has heard the song
    That rolls for aye its (vales) along.
A life beyond, where martyrs sing,
    And ancient prophets hail their King,
While infant cherubs at His feet
    Their voices blend in chorus sweet.

A life beyond—who would not share
    A life so bright, a world so fair?
No sad regret, no parting tears,
    No anxious dread of coming years;
A life beyond, a life of love,
    A world of perfect rest above,
A life where every storm is past—
    O may its joy be ours at last!

Ed. This sheet bears the "CONGRESS" seal embossed in upper left, and there are two
apparent errors in the original. "Pure" in line seven appears as "poor" and "vales" in
stanza two, line four is spelled "vails."
Stanza three has two alterations by the transcriber. In line two, "world" was originally
"home," and "coming" (line four) was "dark. . . ."

12

Fanny Crosby   March 14th, 1876

Dear Savior, make me pure in heart,
  For they Thy face shall see,
And on the bosom of Thy love
  Their rest forever be.

Chorus: Lord, cleanse Thou me from secret faults,
      Let all my life be Thine,
      That I may say and feel the words
      "Thy will be done, not mine."

I do not ask that Thou should'st keep
  My soul from trials free,
But when they come, O let me find
  A hiding place in Thee.
             Chorus.

Thy will in simple, trusting faith,
  Help me Thy will to learn;
And may my heart with fervent love
  And holy ardor burn.
             Chorus.

Be this my one supreme desire—
  To make my calling sure,
To run with joy the Christian race,
  And to the end endure.
             Chorus.

Ed. In this instance (and in all the manuscripts from 1875 and 1876) the name and date appear at the top of the page in the same fine, sweeping hand as the rest of the words. The "CONGRESS" seal is embossed at the upper left of this page.

13

Fanny Crosby   March 27th, 1876

How bright with song, how full of joy
   Our merry festive day,
And while the moments one by one
   In beauty glide away—

Chorus: Once more a happy chorus join,
      Ring out, each heart and voice!
      Exalt our one triumphant Lord,
      And in His name rejoice.

Today the springs of true delight
   Are flowing pure and clear;
Today will be a sunny spot
   Through many a coming year.
          Chorus.

And now, beneath the glowing sky
   Of this our native land,
Let each resolve, for Christ the Lord,
   Like heroes brave to stand.
          Chorus.

"All hail the banner of the cross,"
   Our parting song shall be;
"All hail the banner of the cross,
   For Christ has made us free."
          Chorus.

14

F.J.C.　Apr. 18/76

He Alone

Sinner, throw thy works away,
　Christ alone can save thee;
Now for pardoning mercy pray,
　Christ alone can save thee.

Chorus:　Precious was the life He gave
　　To redeem thee from the grave;
　　Look to Him, O look to Him,
　　He alone can save thee.

He thy sacrifice was made,
　Christ alone can save thee;
On His head thy sins were laid,
　Christ alone can save thee.
　　　　　　　　Chorus.

Come, unworthy as thou art,
　Christ alone can save thee;
Why withhold from Him thy heart?
　Christ alone can save thee.
　　　　　　　　Chorus.

Soon His voice will call no more,
　Christ alone can save thee;
Then thy season will be o'er,
　Christ alone can save thee.
　　　　　　　　Chorus.

Ed.　The right margin has the pencil notation "f f d c B f" at the end of the first stanza—probably a suggestion of a melodic motive. The title is also in pencil, probably by the same person. The "CONGRESS" embossing is at the upper left.

15

F.J.C.   June 9/76

'Tis not so far to yonder clime
  Where angel choirs are singing,
And golden fruits of endless joy
  From life's fair tree are springing.

Chorus: 'Tis not so far; for here we see
      Bright visions of its glory;
      And O, how sweet, when we get there,
      To tell redemption's story.

'Tis not so far to reach the strand
  And scale those heights of pleasure,
Whose length, and breadth, and boundless range
  No finite mind can measure.
                    Chorus.

'Tis not so far to yonder clime
  Where hearts no more shall sever,
And love's unbroken tide of song
  Rolls on and on forever.
                    Chorus.

O, when the white-robed angel Death
  Shall spread his pinions o'er us,
Our souls shall catch the radiant smile
  Of dear ones there before us.
                    Chorus.

Ed.   It is interesting to note that Fanny's death-angel was "white-robed" (last stanza)—
unless this was an error by the *amanuensis*. The sheet carries the embossed "CON-
GRESS" seal.

16

By F. J. Crosby–Sept. 6, 1876

We have news, good news of the promised land,
  Where the oldtime saints in their white robes stand,
With the harps they tuned when the Savior's birth
  Was a welcome song to the listening earth.

Chorus: Will you come with us to the gates of gold
      That open now for the young and old?
      Will you come with us to that land, and share
      In the blest reward of the faithful there?

We have heard of fruits that forever grow
  'Neath the cloudless skies that in beauty glow;
We have heard of songs that forever glide
  O'er the stream of life on the silver tide.
            Chorus.

We are bound for home where the martyrs sing,
  And the kings of earth shall their glory bring,
And the Lord himself, with a loving hand,
  Will direct His own to the promised land.
            Chorus.

We are bound for home; we are strangers here,
  But our hope is strong and our faith is clear;
And we look away to our home so fair,
  And we know by grace we shall enter there.
            Chorus.

Ed.   The page carries the embossed seal "NOLIA MILLS."

17

F. J. Crosby   Sept. 7th, 1876

He shall reign and reign forever,
    Christ our Saviour, brother, friend;
Everlasting is His kingdom,
    His dominion hath no end.

Chorus: Hallelujah, Hallelujah!
          Glory, glory to His name!
          Countless myriads shall adore Him,
          Endless years His work proclaim.

He shall reign and reign forever,
    All the world His praise shall sing,
And the regions now in darkness
    Shall to Him their homage bring.
                        Chorus.

Soon will dawn a glorious morrow;
    Soon will come the promised day,
When from every tribe and kindred
    Shall be heard the joyful lay.
                        Chorus.

Ed.   The manuscript is a partial sheet, 8½″ x 11¼″, torn across the bottom. There is a very
      sharp embossed seal "NOLIA MILLS" at upper left. At lower right the letters "Clh"
      appear—it may have been intended to be "Cho."

18

F. J. Crosby   Nov. 28, 1876

One in Him, our great deliverer,
  Let our hopes and aims be one;
Let us live in sweet communion
  With the Father through the (Son.)

Chorus: Keep the unity of spirit
          In the sacred bonds of peace,
          Strong in Him whose hand will guide us
          In the path of perfect peace.

Like the dew from Hermon falling,
  Like the oil on Aaron's head,
Will the grace of Him, who loves us,
  On his faithful ones descend.
                    Chorus.

One in Him, our dear redeemer,
  Let our prayers as one ascend,
While we add to each petition—
  "Father, let Thy will be done."
                    Chorus.

Ed.   The final word of the first stanza appears as "sun"—no doubt an error. Upper left has
      the "CONGRESS" seal.

19

(mount)
There's a Rock that stands like a tower sublime—
(That Rock)
  Its name is the Rock of Ages;
            (from the cares)
Till the pilgrims rest in the vale of time,
  (His)
  There hope is the Rock of Ages.

Chorus: Oh, build on the Rock, the strong high Rock,
            Oh, build on the Rock of Ages;
            We shall heed not the storm nor the thunder's shock,
            While safe on the Rock of Ages.

We will trust no more to the treacherous sand,
  (flee to)
  But trust in the Rock of Ages;
  (will)   (shall ever)
We shall build a house that for aye shall stand,
  A house on the Rock of Ages.
                  Chorus.

Though the floods may come and the winds may blow,
  Yet calm on the Rock of Ages
        (look on)   (waves below)
We'll sit and drink from the springs that flow,
  (Secure on)
  So cool from the Rock of Ages.
                  Chorus.

             (safe)
We will sing for joy in that dear retreat,
  Our home on the Rock of Ages;
  (lay our souls)   (the)
We will sing for joy at our Saviour's feet,
  For He is the Rock of Ages.
                  Chorus.

Ed.   This is the first manuscript with a folio number—779. Evidently more than 700 hymns
      had been submitted between 1864 and 1877. The full lines are the original manuscript;
      the inter-linear additions evidently suggested editorial changes. At the top of the sheet
      is the name "Sherwin(?)"—probably William F. Sherwin, composer of the tunes
      CHAUTAUQUA and BREAD OF LIFE.
      On the back is the notation "All paid for—$10." From what we know about Fanny
      Crosby's fees, this may have been the amount paid the composer.

806

Lord, Here Am I

Master, Thou callest,
   I gladly obey;
Only direct me,
   And I will away.
Teach me the mission
   Appointed for me,
What is my labor,
   And where it shall be.

Chorus: Master, Thou callest
           And this I reply,
           "Ready and willing,
           Lord, here am I."

Willing, my Savior,
   To take up Thy cross;
Willing to suffer
   Reproaches and loss.
Willing to follow,
   If Thou wilt but lead;
Only support me
   With grace in my need.
                   Chorus.

Ready to labor,
   While life shall remain;
Ready for trials,
   Affliction or pain;
Ready to witness,
   My Savior, for Thee;
Ready to publish
   Thy mercy to me.
                   Chorus.

Living or dying,
   I still would be Thine;
Yet I am mortal
   While Thou art divine.
Pardon, whenever
   I turn from the right;
Pity, and bring me
   Again to the light.
                    Chorus.

                    Fanny Crosby
                  Aug. 15th, 1877

Ed.   The "CONGRESS" seal appears on the original.

21

814

Light Over Yonder

How oft in the midst of the darkness,
    That hangs o'er the valley of tears,
Through clouds and the mist that surround us,
    The bow of God's mercy appears.

Chorus: O we think of the Light over yonder,
        Whose brightness all other excels;
        There sweetly as ages roll onward,
        The song of eternity swells.

A beam from the Light over yonder,
    Makes lovely the loneliest spot;
It shines when our earth joys have faded,
    The world comprehendeth it not.
        Chorus.

Our bark may be lashed by the billows,
    Its sails may be torn by the blast;
But, cheered by the Light over yonder,
    We'll reach the dear Haven at last.
        Chorus.

O soon, 'neath the sweet-scented branches,
    Whose fruits are immortal and fair;
We'll sit in the Light over yonder,
    And dwell with the glorified there.
        Chorus.

Fanny Crosby
Sept. 13th, 1877
Biglow & Main

Ed.   The third line of the chorus was first written "And ever as ages. . ." and then changed
by the transcriber.

The Whisper of Love

I cannot be sad if my Savior is near,
　He bids all my sadness depart;
I cannot be lonely, if gently I hear
　His whisper of love in my heart.

Chorus:　The whisper of love, soft whisper of love,
　　　　How oft, like the poor wandering dove,
　　　　I fly to the ark with my Savior to rest,
　　　　And hear His soft whisper of love.

I cannot be weary; the days are not long,
　If onward I trustingly move;
And oft on my journey I pause in my song,
　To hear the soft whisper of love.
　　　　　　Chorus.

And when, from the path He has taught me to tread,
　My footsteps forgetfully rove;
How kindly again to that path I am led,
　And cheered by the whisper of love.
　　　　　　Chorus.

No voice in the world is so tenderly sweet,
　No charm can my sorrow remove;
No accents in glory my joy would complete,
　Without the soft whisper of love.
　　　　　　Chorus.

　　　　　　　　　Fanny Crosby
　　　　　　　　　Oct. 23d, 1877

Ed.　This was written on a sheet of ledger paper.

23

889

Hosanna

Hosanna to Jesus, our Savior and King,
  To Jesus, the mighty to save.
The legions of darkness He captive hath led,
  And opened the door of the grave.

Chorus: Hosanna! Hosanna! all glory to Him
      Who comes in the name of the Lord!
      Through whom is salvation to all that believe,
      And trust in His life-giving word.

The kingdoms of earth shall be crumbled to dust,
  Their thrones and their splendor shall fall;
But Jesus, exalted forever, shall reign
  Creator and Monarch of all.
              Chorus.

"Hosanna to Jesus"—sound it abroad,
  His wonderful mercy make known,
That every poor wanderer away from the fold
  May come, and be saved at His throne.
              Chorus.

Fanny Crosby
Jan. 10th, 1878
Biglow & Main

I Will Praise Thee

I will praise Thee, O my Savior,
   I will magnify Thy name;
Yea, my heart and tongue rejoicing,
   Thy salvation shall proclaim.

Chorus: For Thy gift by faith that saves me,
      Precious gift of grace so free,
      Shall my soul pour out its fulness
      In a grateful song to Thee.

I will praise Thee, O my Savior,
   And Thy wondrous love recall;
Thou (hast) covered my transgressions
   By Thy offering once for all.
              Chorus.

Thou hast covered my transgressions
   With Thy righteousness divine,
Through Thy mercy I was pardoned,
   Cleansed, and made a child of Thine.
              Chorus.

I will praise Thee, O my Savior,
   Till my mortal powers shall fail;
Then in nobler strains I'll praise Thee
   When I anchor in the vale.
              Chorus.

Fanny Crosby
Sept. 25th, 1878
B. & M.

Ed.   The original was written on a sheet of ledger paper 7¾″ x 12½″. In the second stanza, third line, the word "hast" appears as "has."

25

Be Not Faithless

Be not faithless, but believe
    Every promise of the Lord;
What ye ask ye shall receive,
    Is the language of His Word.

    Chorus: Though with tears our cup He fill,
                Shall our wayward hearts rebel?
                No! be this our comfort still—
                With the righteous it is well.

Be not faithless—trust and pray;
    On His love O rest secure.
If His Spirit guide our way;
    Can we not its storms endure?
                Chorus.

Be not faithless, if His eye
    Marks the tiny sparrow's fall,
If He hears the raven's cry,
    Will He spurn His children's call?
                Chorus.

Be not faithless, though His face
    He may hide a little while,
He will cheer us with His grace
    And the sunshine of His smile.
                Chorus.

                                    Fanny Crosby
                                    Nov. 27th, 1878

1333

The Half I Cannot Tell

My heart is overflowing
 With gratitude and praise,
To Him whose loving kindness
 Has followed all my days;
To Him who gently leads me
 By cool and quiet rills,
And with their balm of comfort
 My thirsty spirit fills.

Chorus: I feign would tell the story,
    And yet I know full well
    The half was never, never told—
    The half I cannot tell.

Within the vale of blessing,
 I walk beneath the light
Reflected from His glory,
 That shines forever bright.
I feel His constant presence
 Wherever I may be;
How manifold His goodness,
 How rich His grace to me!
        Chorus.

My heart is overflowing
 With love and joy and song,
As if it heard an echo
 From yonder ransomed throng;
Its every chord is vocal
 With music's sweetest lay;
And to its home of sunshine
 It longs to fly away.
        Chorus.

                Fanny ?

Ed. Some editor has altered the last four lines to read:
       And while each chord is thrilling
        With music's sweetest lay,
      To yonder home of sunshine
        In thought I soar away.
     The questioning acknowledgement "Fanny ?" has also been added, and the Biglow &
     Main stamp on the back is dated "Sept. 13, 1879."

27

A Cry for Light

From the palmy isles of the far away,
  From the spicy groves in their bloom arrayed,
Where the heathen bow, and their homage pay
  At the gilded shrines that their hands have made,

> *Chorus:*   There's a call for help and a cry for light,
>   By the surges borne o'er the heaving main,
>   From the souls that grope in a rayless night
>   For the lamp of grace they have sought in vain.

They are turning now, and they stretch their hands
  To the favored clime of the free and brave.
How they plead with us to remove their bands,
  While they ask for Him who alone can save.
                    Chorus.

With a feeling heart and a gen'rous hand,
  With an earnest faith and a fervent prayer,
We will send them aid from our own dear land,
  That will plant the cross of the Savior there.
                    Chorus.

They shall drink ere long of the living spring,
  For the day will come, and its dawn is near,
When the song of praise and of joy shall ring,
  And the utmost bounds of the world shall hear.
                    Chorus.

Fanny J. Crosby
Mch. 3/81

Ed.   This poem appeared on both sides of a sheet of ruled Biglow & Main stationery.

Happy As Happy Can Be

Thy banner of love is o'er me,
   Thy righteousness covers my sin,
My banquet a feast of blessings,
   Refreshing my spirit within.

Chorus: Thus onward I go, rejoicing,
         And trusting, my Savior, in Thee,
         While all the long day I'm singing,
         As happy as happy can be.

Thy banner of love is o'er me,
   I walk in its soul-cheering light,
That shines when my path is darkest,
   Like stars on the brow of the night.
               Chorus.

Thy banner of love is o'er me,
   My shield when the tempter is near;
Thy banner of love is o'er me,
   And so I have nothing to fear.
               Chorus.

Thy banner of love is o'er me,
   And when my life's journey shall close,
'Twill circle my head in glory,
   And wave o'er eternal repose.
               Chorus.

             F.J.C.   April 6th, 1881

Ed.   The copy is typed in small capital letters, and the name and date are penned. The sheet has been torn across the bottom and has red and blue ledger lines from top to bottom about 1½ inches from the left side.

29

1443

The Love That Brought Us There

O the height and depth of mercy,
  O the length and breadth of love,
O the fullness of redemption
  Thro' our great High Priest above;
Who Himself was made an offering
  For the sins of all our race,
And for every true believer
  Has prepared in heaven a place.

Chorus: When our eyes behold the glory
           Of His Kingdom, bright and fair,
           We shall never cease to wonder
           At the love that brought us there.

O, the harps, that now exalting
  From the mount of Zion ring;
O, the song of holy rapture
  Which the ransomed army sing;
Yes, the ransomed who have conquered,
  They have crossed the swelling flood;
And their garments, pure and spotless,
  [Are made white in Jesus' blood.]
                    Chorus.

Praise the Lord for this redemption!
  Praise the Lord, that all may come,
And be heirs of life eternal
  In our Father's blessed home;
Where no throb of pain or sorrow
  Will disturb the tranquil breast,
Where the sower and the reaper
  From their toil shall sweetly rest.
                    Chorus.

                              F.J.C.
                    Apl (sic) 23d, 1881

Ed.   The first three lines of this hymn appear in the refrain of "Take the World, but Give Me
       Jesus"—a song written by Fanny Crosby to music of John R. Sweney and published in
       1879.
       The last line of stanza two is completely missing, and has been supplied by this editor.

1657

Do Good

Do good, do good with a cheerful heart
  And a kind and ready hand,
'Tis a maxim taught by the wise and great,
  'Tis the Lord's divine command.

Chorus: Do good in the name of Him who came
        To die for the sins of man;
        Let the golden rule of our lives be this—
        Do all the good we can.

Do good, do good; if we have the will
  We can always find the way;
Let us make the best of our moments here,
  For we have not long to stay.
          Chorus.

Do good, do good while the light remains,
  For the day will soon be o'er;
And the night will come with shadows dark,
  When the time for work is o'er.
          Chorus.

Do good, do good from a sense of love
  That we feel to Christ our Lord,
And the smallest thing that we do for Him
  Will receive its own reward.
          Chorus.

Fanny Crosby
Oct. 6/82

Ed. The top of the original sheet bears a rubber stamp: Biglow & Main, Oct. 7, 1892, 76 East 9th St., N.Y., and the embossed "CONGRESS" seal at upper left.

31

1696

Speak Lovingly

Speak lovingly and kindly,
　　While here on earth we stay;
Our life is but a shadow
　　That soon will glide away.

Chorus:　One little word of kindness
　　　　On some poor heart may fall,
　　　　Like beams from yonder golden sun
　　　　That brightly shines for all.

Speak lovingly and kindly;
　　O let the task be ours
To scatter by the wayside—
　　Not thorns, but smiling flowers.
　　　　　　　Chorus.

Though crowned with peace and plenty
　　Our happy homes may be,
Remember those around us
　　Less favored far than we.
　　　　　　　Chorus.

Speak lovingly and kindly;
　　For He our Lord, we know,
To us will show the kindness
　　That we to others show.
　　　　　　　Chorus.

Fanny Crosby
Dec. 6th, 1882

Ed.　The embossed "CONGRESS" seal appears on the page.

1738

Plead with the Souls that Perish

Plead with the souls that perish,
   Weep for the guilt-oppressed,
Under the yoke of bondage,
   Out of the ark of rest.
Tell of the sheep that wandered
   Out on the mountains cold,
Tell how the Shepherd brought it
   Home to the sacred fold.

Chorus: Plead with the souls that perish,
            Weep for the guilt-oppressed,
            Under the yoke of bondage,
            Out of the ark of rest.

Plead with the souls that perish,
   Lead them to mercy's door,
There at the cross beside them
   Pray for them o'er and o'er.
Urge them to come to Jesus,
   Draw them by words of love,
Think not the work before you
   Fruitless or vain will prove.
                  Chorus.

Plead with the souls that perish,
   Labor the lost to win;
Tell them the blood of Jesus
   Cleanseth from every sin.
Plead with a faith unshaken,
   Jesus will hear your plea,
Trust in the golden promise—
   "Great will the harvest be."
                  Chorus.

F. J. Crosby
Feb. 21st, 1883

Ed.   The manuscript carries the "CONGRESS" seal.

33

1773

Walk in the Footsteps of Jesus

Walk in the footsteps of Jesus,
  Follow the lamp of His life,
Not at a distance, but closely,
  Lest we should turn from the right.

Chorus: Follow Him nearer and nearer,
       Go where He patiently trod,
       Seeking and saving the lost ones,
       Leading them homeward to God.

Walk in the footsteps of Jesus,
  (Always) so loving and kind,
Lifting the shadows before Him,
  Leaving a blessing behind.
             Chorus.

Walk in the footsteps of Jesus,
  Learning our duty to know;
Learning by faith and submission
  More of His spirit to show.
             Chorus.

Gather the words He has spoken,
  Gather the truths they impart;
Bind them like jewels about us,
  Treasure them deep in the heart.
             Chorus.

Fanny Crosby
May 9th, 1883

Ed.   The original manuscript has the sharpest impression of the "CONGRESS" seal. In
stanza two, line two, the first word appears as "alway."

1832

God's Great Love for Me

Out of the mist that gathers,
    Where doubt and fear I see,
Into the broad, bright sunshine
    Of God's great love to me;
Out of my heart repinings
    And all my vain desires,
Into the calm submission
    A childlike trust inspires.

    Chorus: Out of the mist that gathers,
            Where doubt and fear I see,
            Into the broad, bright sunshine
            Of God's great love to me.

Out of my pride and envy,
    My wayward thoughts that rise,
Into the patient meekness
    That grace alone supplies.
Out of a murmuring spirit,
    Whose wants are never still,
Into a perfect resting
    In God my Father's will.
                    Chorus.

Out of whate'er would keep me
    From holy joys away,
Out of whate'er would hinder
    My progress day by day;
Out of myself uplifted,
    From all its boasting free;
Close to the cross of Jesus,
    O, there my soul would be.
                    Chorus.

Fanny Crosby
Sept. 20th, 1883

35

1967

A Refuge in Thee

When hopes that are brightest
  Like autumn have flown,
When hearts that we treasured
  Have left us alone,
O, where from the sadness
  Of grief should we flee,
If faith had no refuge,
  Dear Savior, in Thee?

Chorus: There we may rest,
          Sheltered and blest,
          Safe and forever—
          O there we may rest.

When dark are the storm clouds
  Above us that roll,
And wild are the surges
  That break o'er the soul,
O, where from the tempest
  Of life should we flee,
If faith had no refuge,
  Dear Savior, in Thee?
                            Chorus.

Though faith may be tested
  And love may be tried,
How peaceful the haven
  [Where] all may abide;
Whate'er with the tempter
  Our conflict may be,
We still have a refuge,
  Dear Savior, in Thee.
                            Chorus.

Fannie Crosby
Oct. 15th, 1884

Ed. The paper has the embossed seal, "CONGRESS." In stanza two, the first word of the
     second line was originally "Around" and was crossed out and "Above" written over it.
     We have also added a word in stanza three to make both the sense and the meter
     complete.

2080

Savior Divine

Come to my waiting heart,
  Savior divine;
Spring of its life Thou art,
  O Savior mine.

Chorus: Reach down Thy hand to me,
           Lift up my soul to Thee;
           Thine shall the glory be,
           O Savior mine.

More of Thy grace I need,
  Savior divine;
Now for that grace I plead,
  O Savior mine.
                              Chorus.

Come and my doubts remove,
  Savior divine;
Grant me Thy perfect love,
  O Savior mine.
                              Chorus.

                              Fanny J. Crosby
                              May 13th, 1885

Ed.   This poem appears on the back of a letterhead with this printed heading:
                    Biglow & Main
              (Successors to Wm. B. Bradbury)
            Publishers of Church and Sunday School Music
         76 East Ninth St., N.Y., and 81 Randolph St., Chicago.
      There is an incomplete watermark: "L L . . . Paper . . ."

37

Thus Far

Thus far Thy hand has brought us,
  Dear Savior, on our way;
Thus far Thy tender mercy
  Has crowned each fleeting day.

Chorus: Thus far Thy hand has brought us,
          And still we trust in Thee;
          O help our grateful, loving hearts
          Obedient still to be.

Thus far Thy hand has brought us
  Through trials strong and deep;
Thy voice has stilled the tempest,
  And lulled the waves to sleep.
                Chorus.

How oft Thy words have cheered us
  In dark temptation's hour;
How oft, amid their weakness,
  Our souls have felt Thy power.
                Chorus.

We'll trust in every danger,
  We'll trust, though surges roar;
We'll trust, till safely anchored
  On yonder peaceful shore.
                Chorus.

Fanny Crosby
Oct. 15th, 1885

Ed.   The manuscript bears the embossed "CONGRESS" seal. Originally, the second line, fourth stanza read "We'll trust till life is o'er."

2318

Arise! Go Forth!

Arise! gird on our armor!
  Arise! go forth today,
And bear the royal standard
  Along the King's highway.
He claims the willing service
  Our youthful hearts can give;
His love demands the promise
  That we for Him will live.

Chorus: Arise! gird on our armor!
            Arise! go forth today,
            And bear the royal standard
            Along the King's highway.

Arise! go forth, believing
  Through Him we shall prevail.
If His right hand uphold us,
  There's no such word as "fail."
If He our Lord be with us,
  Our buckler, strength, and shield,
Not all the tempter's legions
  Can drive us from the field.
                Chorus.

Arise! go forth rejoicing
  To reach the countless throng,
Whose victor palms are waving
  In yonder land of song.
Go forth like them to conquer,
  And when our crown is won,
We'll hear the Savior's welcome,
  "O blest of God, well done!"
                Chorus.

Fanny Crosby
Mar. 17th, 1887

Ed.   The sheet carries the embossed word "Favorite."

2341

His Face I Yet Shall See

I know in whom my soul believes,
  I know in whom I trust;
My faith is anchored on His word,
  Because its laws are just.

Chorus: I know that my Redeemer lives!
  O blessed thought to me—
  That, in His righteousness arrayed,
  His face I yet shall see.

I know 'tis my Redeemer's will
  That I the cross should bear;
I know from Him my heart receives
  The bliss of answered prayer.
                    Chorus.

I know 'tis my Redeemer's hand
  That marks the path I tread;
I know that on His arm of love
  He leans my weary head.
                    Chorus.

I know the time will not be long
  Till He shall bid me come,
And share, with all the ransomed ones,
  Eternal rest at home.
                    Chorus.

Fanny Crosby
June 9th, 1887

2346

Worship the Lord with Gladness

God loveth the meek and lowly
  Who seek Him by faith and prayer;
He dwells with the contrite spirit,
  And maketh His temple there.

Chorus: Then worship the Lord with gladness;
  Sing praise to His name divine!
  For they who in wisdom obey Him,
  Like stars in His crown will shine.

God loveth the earnest-hearted
  Who care for His wandering sheep,
And over the cold, dark mountains
  A tireless watch they keep.
                              Chorus.

God loveth the patient reapers
  That labor till set of sun;
That gather their sheaves rejoicing,
  Nor rest till their work is done.
                              Chorus.

Fanny Crosby
June 16th, 1887

41

Hallelujah! Hallelujah!

Soft and still the breeze that murmured
  'Round the place where Jesus lay,
Not a whisper broke the silence
  Till the stone was rolled away.
Then the powers of darkness trembled,
  Then their host in terror fled;
Flinty rocks were rent asunder,
  For the tomb gave up its dead.

Refrain: Hallelujah! Hallelujah!
       All our doubts and fears have fled.
       Hallelujah! Hallelujah!
       Christ hath risen from the dead.

Blessed day of consolation,
  Glorious day of hope divine,
From the cross of pain and anguish
  See the star of mercy shine.
Heaven and earth, rejoice together,
  While the feast of love we keep,
And away, in far off regions,
  Deep is calling unto deep.
                    Chorus.

Open wide our hearts to Jesus—
  Let us hear His voice anew,
While today our guest He enters,
  Saying, "Peace be unto you."
Open wide our hearts to Jesus—
  In His temple, while we meet,
May devotion pure and sacred
  Make the soul's communion sweet.
                    Chorus.

Fanny Crosby
Jan. 13th, 1888

Ed.   Part of the folio number is missing from the original. The last two numbers are "78,"
      and we surmise it was "2378."

2391

Labor and Trust and Pray

Into the fold of the Shepherd
  Gather the poor and the weak;
Teach them the way of salvation,
  Urge them its blessing to seek.

Chorus: Work with the dawn of the morning,
  Work till the close of the day,
  Work while the life-lamp is burning,
  Labor and trust and pray.

Work for the lost and neglected;
  Out on the mountains they roam,
Far from the shelter of mercy,
  Exiled from God and from home.
    Chorus.

Carry the message of gladness;
  Haste, and your mission fulfill.
Why should you faint or grow weary?
  Jesus will comfort you still.
    Chorus.

Pray and your prayer will be answered;
  Trust, and your eyes shall behold
Lost ones to Jesus returning,
  Gathered and safe in His fold.
    Chorus.

Fanny Crosby
Mar. 15th, 1888

Ed.   The 8″ x 9½″ sheet, on which this appears, is lined in squares.

43

2464

Forever at Rest

I know there's a beautiful mansion
  In glory preparing for me,
And there, with my blessed Redeemer,
  Forever at rest I shall be.

Chorus: Home, home, beautiful home,
    That oft in a vision I see;
    O, there, with my blessed Redeemer,
    Forever at rest I shall be.

I think of the loved ones departed,
  Whose trials and crosses are o'er;
I think of their bliss when they anchored,
  And knew they were safe on the shore.
          Chorus.

Of labor I would not be weary,
  At sorrow I would not repine;
But say, in the words of the Master,
  "Thy will, O my Father, be mine."
          Chorus.

I know that the time is approaching,
  I know that it will not be long,
Till I shall be one of the number
  To learn and to sing the New Song.
          Chorus.

Ed. The original manuscript carries no name. The page has a rubber-stamp figure of a comic-strip-style policeman and the initial P.—in red ink. Obviously there was a second initial, but it is not complete enough to decipher.

2771

Like the Waters of the Sea

O, the time is fast approaching,
  When our Great and Glorious King
Out of every clime and nation
  All His ransomed ones shall bring.

Chorus: When proclaimed to every land
       Shall the gospel message be,
       And shall overspread the earth
       Like the waters of the sea.

Then the name of our Redeemer
  Will resound from shore to shore,
In a shout of joy and gladness
  That was never heard before.
  (Such as ne'er was heard before.)
            Chorus.

O, the time is fast approaching,
  And it may be very near,
When the Savior in His glory
  With the angels shall appear.
            Chorus.

Then be faithful, O be faithful,
  And obedient to His word;
And be sure that we are ready
  (May our eyes be ever looking)
For the coming of the Lord.
            Chorus.

Fanny Crosby
April 23d, 1890

Ed. At the bottom of the page is a scrawl that seems to read: "O.K. Considering. I.A.S." (I.
   Allan Sankey.) The same hand evidently penciled in the changes that appear in
   parentheses. There is a faint embossed seal which seems to be "Hamilton."

45

3022

He Was a Man of Sorrows

Never a tear of sadness
   That into our lives may fall,
Never a throb of anguish
   But Jesus hath known it all;
Never a broken spirit
   Sought vainly in Him relief,
He was a man of sorrows,
   And He was acquaint (sic) with grief.

Chorus: He was a man of sorrows,
      Many the tears He wept;
      He was a lonely watcher,
      Praying while others slept.

Never a thorn that pierceth
   Our tired and aching feet,
Never a cross we carry,
   And never a storm we meet;
Never a contrite mourner
   His pity will not behold,
Never a heart forsaken
   His mercy will not enfold.
             Chorus.

Never a seed we scatter
   That falls to the earth in vain,
Never His love refuseth
   The early and latter rain;
Never a deed of kindness
   For Jesus, our blessed Lord,
Never a cup of water
   But bringeth its own reward.
             Chorus.

Fanny Crosby
Jan. 29, 1891

Ed.   The beginning line was first written "Never a drop...." We have not changed the doubtful word "acquaint" in the last line, first stanza, in order to keep the meter uniform in all stanzas. The seal "HAMILTON" is embossed at lower right.

3023

The Word of the Lord

The word of the Lord is perfect,
And happy are they that hear;
It storeth the heart with knowledge
That shines like the noonday clear,
The word of the Lord is perfect;
The word of the Lord is pure;
And they, who in faith receive it,
Have anchored their hope secure.

The word of the Lord is perfect,
And thus it converts the soul;
The numberless worlds created
Are under its vast control.
The word of the Lord is mighty;
Forever its truth shall stand;
It speaks, and the winds and waters
Are stilled at its high command.

The word of the Lord is earnest,
Admitting of no delay;
It counsels, persuades, and urges
To come and be saved today.
The word of the Lord is precious;
The word of the Lord is love;
It tells of a life through Jesus,
A home and a rest above.

Fanny Crosby
Feb. 2nd, 1891

47

Forever and Forever

Forever and forever
　With Thee, my all in all,
Beneath eternal sunshine
　On which no shadows fall.

Chorus:　O joy, all joy excelling,
　　　　O deep, unbounded love,
　　　　That for Thine own provided
　　　　Such blessed things above.

Forever and forever
　To know my work is done,
My humble sheaves accepted,
　My crown of promise won.
　　　　　　　Chorus.

Forever and forever
　To sing redeeming grace,
And see my Father's image
　Reflected in Thy face.
　　　　　　　Chorus.

Forever and forever—
　O Savior, can it be
That such a weight of glory
　Thou hast prepared for me?
　　　　　　　Chorus.

Fanny Crosby
Feb. 3rd, 1891

3041

Thine the Praise!

Like the bird that sings at morning
   When it ushers in the day,
Thus my heart, to Thee uplifted,
   Sings aloud its grateful lay.

Chorus: O my Savior, through Thy Spirit
         Thou hast led me all my days;
         Thou hast crowned my life with mercy—
         Thine the glory, Thine the praise!

Though the clouds may sometimes gather,
   And through storms my path may be,
Yet I hear Thy voice above me,
   And Thy ruling hand I see.
               Chorus.

When these fleeting scenes are ended,
   And to earth I bid farewell,
When I reach Thy blessed kingdom,
   Then in nobler strains I'll tell.
               Chorus.

Fanny Crosby
Mar. 12th, 1891

49

3145

Go On

Go on, ye valiant soldiers,
  That march in bright array;
Our Captain is before us,
  His presence cheers our way.

Chorus: Go on, go on,
        Our many foes to meet;
        Keep bright the Christian's armor,
        And never fear defeat.

Go on, ye valiant soldiers;
  And, like an army brave,
Throw out the royal standard,
  And let our colors wave.
                Chorus.

Go on, till death be faithful;
  And when the war is o'er,
White robes and palms in glory
  Are ours forevermore.
                Chorus.

Fanny Crosby
Oct. 30th, 1891

Ed.   The original sheet of paper bears the "CONGRESS" seal embossed, and the watermark
"Platner & Porter. Superfine."

3179

Our Guiding Star

O look not back, but forward;
  For why should memory dwell
On years, to which forever
  Our hearts have said farewell?

Chorus: Press on, the past forgetting,
          Press on to climes afar;
          Press on from grace to glory,
          With hope our guiding star.

O look not back, but forward;
  If we in Christ are one,
No more will He remember
  The wrongs that we have done.
                Chorus.

O look not back, but forward,
  Do good while yet we may;
And then, a golden sunset
  Will crown our closing day.
                Chorus.

Fanny Crosby
Dec. 28th, 1891

Ed.   The seal "HAMILTON" is embossed on the manuscript.

51

3191

Kindly Words

Speak kindly words, whose gentle tones
  May soothe another's woe,
And stay perhaps the silent tears
  That only God can know.

Chorus: A little word, that none can hear
          But those to whom 'tis said,
          May bring a wanderer to the fold,
          And lift a drooping head.

Speak kindly words, for only these
  Will e'er the lost reclaim;
O speak them for the Master's sake,
  And trusting in His name.
                Chorus.

If we but knew the hearts that yearn
  For kindness every day,
From those we pass unheeded now
  We would not turn away.
                Chorus.

Fanny Crosby
Jan. 13th, 1892

Ed.   The "HAMILTON" seal appears at the bottom.

3238

Steadily On

Blessed are they that in good and ill—
  Cheerfully on, steadily on—
Clinging to Jesus, have served Him still,
  Cheerfully, steadily on.
Blessed are they that in faith abound,
  Shedding the sunshine of love around,
Singing the gospel with joy profound,
  Cheerfully, steadily on.

Blessed are they that have toiled for years,
  Cheerfully on, steadily on,
Blessed are they that have sown in tears,
  Cheerfully, steadily on.
They that have silently watched and prayed,
  Tempted, afflicted, but not dismayed;
Patiently trusting through storm and shade,
  Cheerfully, steadily on.

Blessed are they that are toiling still,
  Cheerfully on, steadily on;
Learning and doing the Master's will,
  Cheerfully, steadily on.
Blessed are they that in mansions fair
  Beautiful garments of glory wear,
Blessed are they that are traveling there,
  Cheerfully, steadily on.

Fanny Crosby
Mar. 17th, 1892

Ed.   The original page carries the embossed seal "HAMILTON."

53

3243

My Redeemer

Precious name of my Redeemer—
How it cheers my fainting soul,
When the waves of sorrow gather,
And the clouds above me roll.

Chorus: Name of all on earth the sweetest,
Name of all in heaven most dear;
Whensoe'er in faith I breathe it,
Waves are calm and skies are clear.

Blessed name of my Redeemer—
When my heart is full of care,
And my worldly hopes deceive me,
I can find a refuge there.
Chorus.

Blessed name of my Redeemer—
I will sing it o'er and o'er,
Sing it with the ransomed army,
When this fleeting life is o'er.
Chorus.

Fanny Crosby
Mar. 25th, 1892

Ed.   In this instance, and in several others, the word "chorus" does not appear; instead there
is a wavy line at the left of the second paragraph.
On the back side of this sheet is written: "Justified by faith divine. (Mch 23/92)" The
seal "ISLAND CITY" is embossed.

2381

A Faithful Vigil Keeps

There is a light that shineth
Along our (pilgrim) way,
That fills our hearts with sunshine
When other joys decay.

Chorus: Our Savior, blessed Savior,
            Who slumbers not nor sleeps,
            O'er all our (pilgrim) journey
            A faithful vigil keeps.

There is a light that shineth
When all is lone and drear,
A voice that whispers comfort
In words of happy cheer.
                Chorus.

Then let us never weary,
Nor think our time is long,
But spend each golden moment
In prayer and joyful song.
                Chorus.

Fanny Crosby
May 13, 1892

Ed. The word "pilgrim" appears as "pilgrim's" in both the first stanza and the chorus. It is our guess that Fanny Crosby would agree to our change, or that the *amanuensis* made a mistake.

The manuscript has the embossed seal "FAVORITE" in the upper left corner. Note that the folio number loses its sequence at this point, since the last number was 3243. This number should probably be 3381. The sequence "gets back on the track" with "My Anchor," dated Oct. 27th, 1893.

55

2436

How Wonderful the Story

How wonderful the story,
   Whose words of truth unfold
A love surpassing knowledge,
   Whose depth can ne'er be told;
The love of God the Father
   To sinful men below,
His infinite compassion
   Too great for us to know.

Chorus: We bow our heads with reverence,
             His goodness we adore,
             And praise Him for the mercy
             That saves forevermore.

How wonderful the story
   From angel tongues that rang,
When "glory in the highest"
   O'er Judah's plains they sang.
How wonderful the story
   That woke the dewy morn,
When, cradled in a manger,
   The Prince of peace was born.
                         Chorus.

For us He toiled and labored
   Through long and weary years;
He trod the path of sorrow,
   And bore our griefs and fears.
He gave His life our ransom;
   The world He overcame,
That we, through His atonement,
   Might conquer in His name.
                         Chorus.

Fanny Crosby
July 16th, 1892

2582

Gather the Children

Gather the children, dear Savior,
   Tenderly bring them to Thee;
Led by the voice of Thy Spirit,
   Grant that they early may be.

Chorus: Gather them now, gather them now,
           Never to wander away;
           Into the fold of Thy mercy
           Gather the children today.

Gather the children, dear Savior,
   Into Thy pasture so fair;
Shield them secure from the tempter,
   Keep their young hearts (in) Thy care.
               Chorus.

Gather the children, dear Savior,
   Teach them to honor Thy laws;
Then, with an earnest endeavor,
   Help them to work for Thy cause.
               Chorus.

Fanny Crosby
Mar. 17th, 1893

Ed.   In stanza two, last line, the original is "from Thy care," and is obviously wrong. The
     "HAMILTON" seal is embossed on the upper left.

57

2584

The Children's Flower Song

We are coming, we are coming,
   Like the merry birds we sing;
Pretty roses, fragrant lilies,
   Nature's fairest gifts we bring.

  Chorus: Pretty roses, fragrant lilies,
          Spangled o'er with morning dew,
          Fresh and blooming in their beauty,
          We have gathered them for you.

May the sunshine we have brought you
   With our lovely flowers today,
Whisper softly words of comfort,
   Chasing every cloud away.
               Chorus.

In our Father's blessed Kingdom
   May we meet you by and by,
Where no sickness ever enters,
   Where the roses never die.
               Chorus.

Fanny Crosby
Dec. 28th, 1892

58

2585

We have gathered in the sunshine
Of these golden festal hours;
And how joyful was our meeting
With our teachers, friends and flowers.

We have listened to the echoes
That to memory still are dear,
Little thinking, in our rapture,
Of the parting hour so near.

When our moments seemed the brightest
And of purest pleasure tell,
O, 'tis then we feel the sorrow
Of that lonely word—"farewell."

We have gathered in the sunshine,
And we floated in a dream .
O'er the merry dimpled waters
Of a calmly flowing stream.

We are waking, quickly waking,
For the time has glided by;
And to those we love so fondly
We again must say "goodby."

In that blissful world above us
Where our dear departed dwell,
When we hear our Savior's welcome
We shall never say "farewell"!

Mch. 22/93

Ed. The original is written on the back of company stationery used in the 1880's which has the notation "L. H. Biglow, Surviving Partner." The watermark is evidently "Biglow & Co., New York." The penciled notation "Fanny Crosby?" appears in the upper right corner.

59

2606

My Heart and My Treasure are There

Away in the beautiful home of the blest,
  Beyond the dark shadows of care,
Where sorrow is lost in the transport of rest,
  My heart and my treasures are there.

Chorus: By faith I behold the city of gold,
      Its portals wide open that stand;
      O, there shall I sing at the feet of my King,
      And dwell in Immanuel's land.

Away in the beautiful home of the blest,
  Whose skies are so lovely and fair,
Where all in the verdure of summer is dressed,
  Sweet voices are calling me there.
      Chorus.

Away in the beautiful home of the soul,
  Where crowns of rejoicing they wear;
I thirst for the fountains of pleasure that roll,
  What joy, O what joy to be there.
      Chorus.

Fanny Crosby
Apr. 14th, 1893

Ed.   The designation "Chorus" does not appear—but there is a wavy line at the left of the
    second paragraph. Obviously it is intended to be a refrain, since the meter is different.

2709

When Safe within the Vale

I'll sing the praise of Jesus,
  Who bore the cross for me;
His wondrous love so precious,
  My constant theme shall be.

Chorus: I'll sing the praise of Jesus
      Till heart and voice shall fail,
      And then forever praise Him
      When safe within the veil.

I'll sing His praise at morning,
  And in the noonday bright,
I'll sing His praise at evening,
  And in the hush of night.
                    Chorus.

I'll sing the praise of Jesus,
  On whom my hopes depend;
My everlasting portion,
  My best and dearest friend.
                    Chorus.

                    Fanny Crosby
                  Sept. 14th, 1893

Ed.   This was written on personal note paper 5½″ x 8½″ with the watermark "Bankers Linen."

61

2712

Filled with the Light of Thy Smile

Thanks for a rest that remaineth
  After our labor is past;
Thanks for a gathering homeward,
  Lord, in Thy kingdom at last.

Chorus: Here we are strangers and pilgrims,
    Only sojourning awhile;
    Soon we shall wake in Thy likeness,
    Filled with the light of Thy smile.

Thanks for Thy infinite mercy
  Over us all the day long;
Thanks for Thy numberless blessings
  Turning our sadness to song.
          Chorus.

Thanks for the mansions preparing,
  Jesus our Savior, by Thee;
Thanks for the visions of glory
  Thou dost permit us to see.
          Chorus.

Fanny Crosby
Sept. 15th, 1893

Ed. The top of the manuscript has the initials "C.E."—evidently the transcriber. The title
was first written with the ending "his smile" and then changed. The paper has a large
watermark symbol and the words "All Linen."

3635

My Anchor

I have found a place of refuge,
  Where my trembling soul may hide;
I have found a precious Savior,
  And I now am satisfied.

Chorus: Hallelujah to the Lord!
      I have anchored on His word;
      I can shout a free salvation;
      Hallelujah to the Lord!

I have found a place of refuge,
  And my anchor is secure;
It will hold though storms are raging,
  And I know 'tis firm and sure.
              Chorus.

I have found a place of refuge,
  And my song in heaven shall be
Of the all-atoning mercy
  That has ransomed even me.
              Chorus.

Fanny Crosby
Oct. 27th, 1893

Ed.   The original sheet of paper is 5½″ x 8½″; the watermark has the figure of a heron, and the
date 1887. Note that the correct sequence of numbers resumes with this page.

63

3770

Closer to Thee

Blessed Redeemer, still closer to Thee,
  Drawn by Thy spirit of love I would be.
Thou art the refuge and strength of my heart;
  Oh, that I never from Thee may depart.

Chorus: Closer to Thee, closer to Thee,
      Blessed Redeemer, still closer to Thee;
      What is the world or its pleasures to me?
      Thine for eternity, Lord, I would be.

Closer, when brightest my sky may appear;
  Closer, when tempted and burdened with fear;
Closer, when trustful I sit at Thy feet;
  Closer, when trials and crosses I meet.
            Chorus.

Closer, when softly is fading the light;
  Closer, when gathers the darkness of night;
Closer, when anchored at rest I shall be
  Safe in the homeland, forever with Thee.
            Chorus.

Fanny Crosby
March 24, 1894

64

3891

Mine Eyes Shall Behold Him

Mine eyes shall behold in His beauty
My Savior, Redeemer and King;
My soul shall awake in His likeness,
His mercy forever to sing.

Chorus: Yes, mine eyes shall behold Him;
His promise declareth to me
That, if I believe and obey Him,
In glory His face I shall see.

Mine eyes shall behold in His beauty
The King that I worship and love;
A mansion He now is preparing,
A home in His palace above.
Chorus.

And O, when mine eyes shall behold Him,
When humbly I bow at His feet,
How gladly I'll praise and adore Him
For pardon so precious and sweet.
Chorus.

Fanny Crosby
Aug. 10th, 1894

Ed.   This poem was written on the back of a blank invoice of the Biglow & Main Company,
used in the 1890's. It listed *Gospel Hymns No. 5, Gospel Hymns Consolidated—1, 2, 3 &*
4, and *Evangeliums-Lieder* (Gospel Hymns in German.) *Gospel Hymns No. 5* (words
only, paper) sold for $.05 a copy, and the combined edition (1–4) in morocco, with gilt
edges, for $2.50.

65

3899

Sing Glory

The Lord our God is a strong defense,
  A rock in a thirsty land;
His truth has stood through eternal years,
  And still like His throne shall stand.

Chorus: Then praise Him, ye angels,
       His mighty works proclaim!
       Let every thing in heaven and earth
       Sing glory to His name.

The Lord our God is a dwelling place,
  A tower where His own may rest;
And, sheltered there in His watchful care,
  No harm can the soul molest.
              Chorus.

The Lord our God is a sun and shield,
  His grace He will freely give;
And no good thing will His love withhold,
  If faithful to Him we live.
              Chorus.

The Lord our God from our foes will save,
  And keep us beneath His wings;
His sovereign power will the world declare,
  For He is the King of Kings.
              Chorus.

Fanny Crosby
Aug. 16th, 1894

Ed.   The 5″ x 8″ page bears the embossing "HAMILTON."

3937

Bless the Lord, My Soul

O bless the Lord, and praise Him,
  My soul, and all within—
Who pardons thy transgressions,
  And takes away thy sin;
Who crowns thy life with goodness,
  With mercy, love and truth,
Renewing, like the eagle,
  The vigor of thy youth.

O bless the Lord, and praise Him,
  Exalt His holy name!
The joy of His salvation
  With cheerful heart proclaim.
How kind is He, and gracious
  To all the poor, oppressed.
He pities like a father,
  And gives His children rest.

O bless the Lord, and praise Him,
  Ye angel host, that stand
With faces veiled before Him,
  Fulfilling His command.
Bow down, ye saints, with reverence
  While endless ages roll;
Let heaven and earth adore Him—
  O bless the Lord, my soul.

Fanny Crosby
Oct. 26th, 1894

Ed.   The embossed seal "HAMILTON" appears at the bottom right of the manuscript.

67

3955

For Thee

Come, O come to the waters,
  Flowing so boundless and free;
Hear the voice of the Savior,
  Lost one, He calls to thee.

Chorus: Come, come, why wilt thou roam?
        Mercy is boundless and free.
        Come, O come to the fountain,
        Flowing, yes, flowing for thee.

Now the Savior is waiting,
  Waiting thy sins to forgive;
Come to Him, and believing,
  Look, and thy soul shall live.
                Chorus.

Why, O why dost thou linger?
  Though thou (hast) wandered away,
Still He tenderly calls thee;
  Come, and be saved today.
                Chorus.

                    Fanny Crosby
                    Nov. 9th, 1894

Ed.   In the last stanza, the second line appears "Though thou has wandered away" in the
      original.

3958

The Way Before Me

I know not the way before me,
  But Jesus will guide me still;
And so, in His mercy trusting,
  I patiently wait His will.

Chorus: I know not the cares or sorrows
      That into my life may fall,
      But Jesus, my loving Savior,
      Will give me the grace for all.

I know not the way before me,
  But Jesus my Lord is near,
To shelter, protect and keep me;
  Then why should I doubt or fear?
          Chorus.

I know not the way before me,
  But this to my soul is given—
The promise of life eternal,
  A home and a rest in heaven.
          Chorus.

Fanny Crosby
Nov. 16—94

Ed.   The manuscript carries the embossed seal "HAMILTON."

69

4018

Traveler, Haste!

Traveler, haste, the night is coming,
  Clouds hang boding o'er thy soul;
From a wild and trackless desert
  Hear the distant thunders roll.

Chorus: Traveler, haste, no time to linger!
      Backward turn thy weary eyes;
      Haste to gain the Rock of Ages,
      Where thy only refuge lies.

Traveler, haste, the storm approaches!
  Mercy calls, her voice obey!
Angel hands from heaven are waving;
  Wilt thou, heedless, still delay?
          Chorus.

Haste to Him, whose love so tender
  Gave its life upon the tree.
He is waiting, He is pleading;
  In His arms there's room for thee.
          Chorus.

Fanny Crosby
Jan. 18—95

Ed. There seems to be a problem in the last stanza—obviously Christ's love did not expire on the cross! The hymn is written on heavy note-paper, 4½″ x 7⅞″.

4060

From Shore to Shore

Come to me—'twas Jesus said it—
  Heavy laden, sin-oppressed,
Now, with all your weight of sorrow,
  Come, and I will give you rest.

Chorus: He was bruised for our transgressions,
      'Twas for us the cross He bore;
      Now the King and Prince of glory,
      He shall reign from shore to shore.

Take my yoke—'twas Jesus said it—
  Take my yoke and learn of me;
I in heart am meek and lowly,
  And your burden light shall be.
          Chorus.

Hungry souls, 'tis He invites you
  To a feast with earnest call;
Where the bread of life He offers,
  And enough for each and all.
          Chorus.

Ye who thirst—His word declareth—
  They who on His name believe,
From the well of free salvation
  Joy eternal shall receive.
          Chorus.

                                    Fanny

Ed. The lower right corner of the sheet has been torn off. It probably contained the rest of
the name and possibly a date.

71

4105

My Great High Priest Above

I know in whom my soul believes,
    And where its hope relies;
I know the hand that leadeth me,
    And every want supplies.

> *Chorus:*   I know that neither life nor death
>   Can part me from the love
>   Of Christ, my glorious Advocate,
>   My Great High Priest above.

I know His all-sufficient grace
    My longing heart can fill;
I know His everlasting arms
    Are round about me still.
                Chorus.

I know in whom my soul believes,
    And where its trust is stayed;
I know that I shall walk with Him
    In righteousness arrayed.
                Chorus.

And when I gather at His throne,
    With all the ransomed throng,
In strains of joy that ne'er shall end
    I'll sing the glad new song.
                Chorus.

Fanny Crosby
May 2/95

Ed.   Note that Fanny Crosby began another poem (no. 39) with the same first line.

4111

I Cannot Know

I cannot know but through a glass but darkly;
　My longing eyes the heavenly Canaan see.
But I believe the words my Lord has spoken—
　In that dear land there is a rest for me.

I cannot know the transport that awaits me
　Till He shall lift the shadows from my sight;
Till I awake and, in His glorious image,
　Breathe out His praise amid a flood of light.

I cannot know how soon will dawn the morning,
　Whose radiant beams will banish every care;
But I can trust my Savior's blessed promise,
　And watch and wait, till He shall call me there.

O joy untold! O bliss no words can utter!
　O hope that lives and blooms within my soul!
Home, love and rest in that unclouded region
　Will yet be mine while endless ages roll.

Fanny Crosby
May 13/95

Ed.　The first line of the original has a blue-penciled question mark at the end. The
"HAMILTON" seal has been used twice, once on each side of the sheet.

73

4029

Can a Boy Forget His Mother?

Can a boy forget his mother
    Who has watched him from his birth?
Can he lose the sacred image
    Of the dearest friend on earth?
Though the tempter may beguile him,
    And his steps afar may roam,
There'll be one green spot in memory—
    For his mother and his home.

Can a boy forget his mother
    And the evening prayer she said,
When she laid him down so gently
    In his tiny cradle bed?
In the downward path of evil,
    Though his steps afar may roam,
Yet one hallowed link will bind him
    To his mother and his home.

And perhaps her tender pleading
    For the boy she loves so dear,
Through a kind and patient Savior,
    May arrest his sad career.
It may touch a chord long silent,
    Though afar his steps may roam;
It may bring him back repentant
    To his mother and his home.

Fanny Crosby
Oct. 18/95

Ed.   This sentimental poem is characteristic of the late 19th century, and reminiscent of such songs as "Just Before the Battle, Mother" and "Where Is My Boy Tonight?" On the right hand of the manuscript someone has penciled the notation, "Hand to I.D.S."—referring to Ira D. Sankey.

4229

Haste Where the Master Leadeth

Only an act of kindness,
  Only a smile to cheer
Someone whose life is weary,
  Desolate, dark and drear;
Only a word of comfort
  Spoken for Jesus' sake,
Memories that long have slumbered
  Out of their sleep will wake.

Chorus: Go where the Master leadeth,
          Go while the days are bright;
          Work ere the shadows deepen
          Into the silent night.

Only a tear of pity
  Dropped from a loving eye;
Only a hand extended,
  Greeting the passerby;
Only the name of Jesus
  Breathed in a sweet refrain,
Oft may recall a lost one
  Back to the fold again.
                    Chorus.

Only an act of kindness
  Into a heart oppressed,
Comes like the dew that sparkles,
  Falls like a balm of rest.
Only a cup of water,
  Pure from a cooling spring,
Offered in Christian friendship,
  Joy to a soul may bring.
                    Chorus.

F.J.C.   June 1896

Ed.   The refrain's third line was first "Work till..." and then changed to the above. The
paper has a faint impression of the "CONGRESS" embossing.

75

4256

Thyself in Me

Take, O Lord, this heart of mine;
  Consecrate and seal me Thine.
Let me nearer come to Thee;
  O, reflect Thyself in me.

Chorus: Seal me Thine, forever Thine,
        Through Thy precious blood divine;
        This my constant prayer shall be—
        O reflect Thyself in me.

Let my life and all my ways
  Show Thy love, and speak Thy praise;
Whatsoe'er my trials be,
  O, reflect Thyself in me.
              Chorus.

Trusting on through good and ill,
  By Thy grace defended still;
Let me not impatient be,
  O, reflect Thyself in me.
              Chorus.

Ed.   The manuscript sheet bears the embossed seal, "HAMILTON." There was no name
and no date.

4488

Ring Out, Ye Bells

O star, that rose on Judah's plain
 To hail the infant Savior born,
In all thy beauty, smile again,
 And welcome back His advent morn.

Chorus: Ring out, ye bells, in tuneful chime,
  Good will henceforth to every clime.
  Ring out, ye bells, the choral lay
  That fills (our) hearts with joy today.

Come, gentle peace on wings of love;
 And bring, to crown these golden hours,
Sweet floral gems from heights above,
 That live and bloom in Eden's bowers.
  Chorus.

Sing on, ye hosts of angels bright,
 The song that woke the sleeping earth,
When, on that ne'er-forgotten night,
 Your music told Messiah's birth.
  Chorus.

  Fanny Crosby
  July 31/96

Ed.   The final line of the chorus is obviously wrong on the manuscript, beginning "That fills
 out hearts..." The words are written on a scrap of ledger paper.

77

Shout Hallelujah!

Come to the feet of our infant Redeemer,
Come where today in a manger He lies;
Lift up our hearts in a song of devotion,
Let our hosannas with gladness arise.

Chorus: Tell how He came from the throne of His Father,
Came to the world in the likeness of men;
Hail and exalt Him, the Son of the Highest,
Shout hallelujah again and again!

Over the plains and the mountains of Judah
Prophets beheld and His coming foretold;
Sang of the love and compassion that moved Him—
Love that is purer and better than gold.
Chorus.

Come to the feet of our infant Redeemer,
Come in the light of this beautiful morn;
Then, to the hearts of the poor and the lowly,
Carry the tidings that Jesus is born.
Chorus.

Ed.   In the original, the third line of stanza two has one extra syllable, "Sang of the love and
the compassion that moved Him." At the top of the page someone has penciled "Fanny
Crosby?"

4628

On to the Prize

Called of the Father, accepted in Jesus,
    Heirs of salvation, adopted through grace;
Casting aside every weight that would hinder,
    On to the prize at the end of the race.

Chorus: On, with a courage that will not be daunted;
        On, like the eagle that soars to the sun;
        Never give up till our course we have finished;
        Never give up till our crown we have won.

On, though a legion our path may encompass;
    On, though its arrows against us are hurled;
Strong in the strength that will keep us from falling,
    Bearing the standard that truth has unfurled.
                    Chorus.

Leaving the past, and its trials forgetting,
    Forward, still forward, our landmarks we trace;
Lo! in the distance a signal is flashing;
    On to the prize at the end of the race.
                    Chorus.

On! let us hasten from glory to glory,
    Trusting the promise of infinite love;
They that endure to the end and are faithful,
    They shall inhabit the mansions above.
                    Chorus.

Fanny Crosby
Feb. 19/97

Ed.   This was written on a sheet from a ledger, with page numbers 69 and 70 on the two
sides.

79

Sweetest Carols

The Christmas bells are ringing
  As in the olden time;
Again they bear the tidings:
  "Good will to every clime."

Chorus: O blessed, blessed story
           Of Christ, the new-born King!
           Let every heart, rejoicing,
           Its sweetest carol sing.

The Christmas bells are ringing,
  Their music fills the air;
It calls the happy children
  Within the house of prayer.
                 Chorus.

Ring on, ye bells, with gladness!
  And, in Messiah's name,
Free grace and full salvation
  To all the world proclaim.
                 Chorus.

Fanny Crosby
Feb. 25/97

Ed.   The original was written on a sheet of ledger paper, with numbers 105 and 106 on the two sides.

4657 Xmas Carol

Lo! He Comes

Lo! He comes, the promised Savior,
    Bringing peace, good will to earth;
Tell afar the blessed tidings,
    And rejoice with holy mirth.

Chorus: Strike your harps, ye saints, adore Him!
            Sing for joy, ye sons of men!
            Through the birth of our Redeemer,
            Eden lost shall bloom again.

Lo! He comes, the Lord's anointed,
    Angel choirs amid the sky
Fold their wings and shout hosanna,
    Glory be to God on high!
                  Chorus.

Lo! He comes, our Mediator,
    O! the soul-inspiring words;
Lo! He comes, our Priest and Prophet,
    King of Kings and Lord of Lords.
                  Chorus.

Fanny Crosby
Mar. 12/97

Ed.   The poem was penned on a piece of ledger paper, with page numbers 117 and 118 on
the two sides.

81

Our Savior King

No gems of orient splendor,
   Nor incense pure and sweet,
No rich and costly treasures
   We lay at Jesus' feet.

Chorus: By faith—our star—directed,
          Our thankful hearts we bring,
          And praise, with true devotion,
          Our infant Savior King.

Our thoughts behold the manger
   Where once His head was laid,
We see the Prince of glory
   In earthly robes arrayed.
                Chorus.

We hail the light so lovely,
   That crowns the advent day
Of Him who came to save us,
   And take our sins away.
                Chorus.

Fanny Crosby
May 28/97

4754

The Glorious Time

The glorious time is coming
  When war and strife shall cease,
And all shall dwell together
  Beneath the smile of peace.

Chorus: The north, the south, the east, the west,
        Shall join their hands and sing,
          "The Lord our God has ransomed us,
        And He alone is King."

The glorious time is coming—
  Our faith beholds its light—
When sin no more shall triumph,
  For God will speed the right.
               Chorus.

The glorious time is coming,
  Foretold in God's own word,
When every clime and nation
  Shall know and praise the Lord.
               Chorus.

                    Fanny Crosby
                    June 25/97

83

4783

Yet There Is Room

List to the message that comes today—
   Yet there is room.
Jesus is calling, O hear Him say—
   "Yet there is room."

Chorus: Room at the cross where He bowed His head,
        Room at the cross where His blood was shed;
        Room at the feast that for you He spread—
        Yet there is room.

Haste to the fountain so deep and wide;
   Yet there is room.
Bury your sins in its crimson tide;
   Yet there is room.
           Chorus.

Room in the arms of a Savior's love;
   Yet there is room.
Room in His kingdom of life above;
   Yet there is room.
           Chorus.

Fanny Crosby
Aug. 8/97

Ed.   The original manuscript was a torn fragment of ruled paper 6¼″ x 8″ with the watermark
"Platner & Porter Company."

4790

Beautiful Bells

Beautiful bells of Eden fair,
   Chiming at eve on the calm, still air,
Lifting the soul, with its toil oppressed,
   Into the vales of the pure and blest.

Chorus: Beautiful bells, so sweet and clear,
       That oft in a dream I hear;
       Welcome the message they bring to me
       Over the waves of the crystal sea.

Beautiful bells of Eden bright,
   Murmuring on through the hush of night,
Telling my heart of the friends I love,
   Gathered at last in their home above.
                Chorus.

Beautiful bells of Eden's clime,
   Softly they breathe in their tones sublime,
Echoes of joy from a white-robed throng,
   Praising the Lord in a world of song.
                Chorus.

Fanny Crosby
Aug. 13/97

Ed.   The original first line of the chorus was "Sweet beautiful bells so clear"; this was crossed out. In the second stanza, fourth line, the original draft was "Gathered and safe"; the words "at last" were penciled above.

85

For Thy Glory

Only to live for Thy glory,
  Only to know I am Thine,
Close to my heart like a treasure,
  Clasping Thy promise divine;
Only to feel that in sorrow
  Still Thou art caring for me;
Jesus, my blessed Redeemer,
  This my petition shall be.

Only to live for Thy glory,
  Only to wait at Thy throne,
Only to walk in Thy footsteps,
  Led by the Spirit alone;
Only to glean with the reapers
  Fruit of rejoicing for Thee;
Jesus, my blessed Redeemer,
  This my petition shall be.

Only to live for Thy glory,
  Bearing reproach for Thy name,
Willing to do or to suffer,
  If at the last I may claim
One little place in the mansion
  Thou art preparing for me:
Jesus, my blessed Redeemer,
  This my petition shall be.

Fanny Crosby
March 14, 1898

Ed.   The original is one of the few typed copies. The paper has a watermark "Collateral Bond."

4949

Stand Up for the Right

The eyes of the world are upon us;
O Christians, awake and beware!
Look well to our lives every moment,
Be faithful, and watch unto prayer.

Chorus: Avoid the appearance of evil;
The path of the righteous pursue.
Stand up for the right and defend it;
To Jesus be loyal and true.

The eyes of the world are upon us;
Keep close to the side of our Lord.
Remember the perfect example
He left in His excellent word.
Chorus.

The eyes of the world are upon us;
But He, our Redeemer and Friend,
Has promised His own to deliver,
And carry them safe to the end.
Chorus.

Fanny Crosby
Apr. 15/98

87

4950

Let Me Walk in Thee

Light of all who come to Thee,
  Precious light that shines for me,
Let me still Thy glory see—
  Jesus, loving Savior.

Chorus: Jesus, loving Savior,
          Ever dear to me,
          Light of every trusting heart,
          Let me walk in Thee.

Light of life's eternal ray,
  Leading up to endless day,
Guide and cheer my troubled way—
  Jesus, loving Savior.
                    Chorus.

Light of all by sin oppressed,
  Light of faith and hope and rest,
Light, in whom my soul is blest—
  Jesus, loving Savior.
                    Chorus.

                              Fanny Crosby
                              Apr. 15/98

88

5074

Now and Forever

Now and forever, O Father above,
  Praise for Thy mercy, Thy wonderful love;
Now and forever, Thy promise shall stand,
  We are Thy people, the work of Thy hand.

Chorus: Monarch and scepter shall bow at Thy name,
        Nation to nation Thy truth shall proclaim;
        Father, Creator, Redeemer in one,
        Now and forever, Thy will be done.

Now and forever, O Savior divine,
  Honor, dominion and triumph be Thine;
Thou hast redeemed us from death and the grave,
  Now and forever Thy standard shall wave.
          Chorus.

Now and forever our anthems shall rise,
  Joyfully wafted by faith to the skies;
Now and forever the ransomed shall sing,
  "Praise in the highest to Jesus our King."
          Chorus.

Fanny Crosby
Oct. 21, 1902

89

Hear Again

Hear again the bells of evening
  Floating softly through the air;
In the west the light has faded,
  'Tis the hallowed hour of prayer.

Chorus: Angels now their wings are folding,
        While beneath the mercy seat,
        In the bonds of love united,
        Kindred hearts each other greet.

Still again the bells are calling:
  "Sorrow-laden, toil-oppressed,
Lay aside your heavy burdens,
  Jesus waits to give you rest."
              Chorus.

Welcome, hour of sweet communing
  With the Father and the Son,
With the blessed Holy Spirit—
  God eternal, Three in One.
              Chorus.

Fanny Crosby
Nov. 4/98

Ed.   The reverse side of the sheet has the notation: "Return. This is sample for metre."

5116

O Troubled Heart

O troubled heart, why thus repine?
  Canst thou not trust His hand divine,
Who all thy life has been thy stay,
  And (led thee) gently day by day?

Chorus: O grieve Him not with anxious fears
           Of what may come in future years;
           In Him abide, be faithful still,
           And let Him lead thee where He will.

O troubled heart, why thus repine,
  If thou art His, and He is thine?
Then will He not for thee provide?
  What canst thou ask on earth beside?
                Chorus.

O troubled heart, why thus repine,
  Though trials must—and will be thine?
With patient faith believe His word,
  And thou shalt reap a blest reward.
                Chorus.

Fanny Crosby
Nov. 25/98

Ed.   The last line of the first stanza was first written "And lead the. . . ."

91

5118

Come, O Come Away

Dost thou feel the need of Jesus
  In thy soul today?
Where He shed His blood to save thee,
  Come, O come away.

Chorus: There, His throne of grace addressing,
  Unto Him thy sins confessing,
  Thou shalt find a precious blessing,
  Come, O come away.

Now the time by Him accepted,
  Wherefore then delay?
To the cross, thy only refuge,
  Come, O come away.
                    Chorus.

Now His love He freely offers,
  Now His voice obey;
To the cross of thy Redeemer,
  Come, O come away.
                    Chorus.

                    Fanny Crosby
                    Nov. 25/98

5121

Come As Thou Art

Come as thou art, there is no other way;
  Haste, for the angels are chiding thy stay.
Come, and this moment thy soul may be free,
  If thou believest, there's pardon for thee.

Chorus: Pardon for thee, pardon for thee,
    What of thy answer, O what will it be?
    Come, and this moment thy soul may be free,
    List for the promise—there's pardon for thee.

Come as thou art or it may be too late,
  Though the compassion of Jesus is great,
Slight not His mercy or He may depart,
  Come to Him quickly, and come as thou art.
    Chorus.

Why dost thou wait, when He is so near,
  Breathing a message of love in thine ear?
Though thy transgressions like crimson may be,
  If thou repentest, there is pardon for thee.
    Chorus.

Fanny Crosby
Dec. 2/98

Ed. Across the scrap of heavy paper (7¾" x 4¾"), someone has blue-penciled "written to
pardon for thee"!

93

5146

For What His Love Denies

God does not give me all I ask,
  Nor answer as I pray;
But, O, my cup is brimming o'er
  With blessings day by day.
How oft the joy I thought withheld
  Delights my longing eyes,
And so I thank Him from my heart
  For what His love denies.

Sometimes I miss a treasured link
  In friendship's hallowed chain,
And yet His smile is my reward
  For every throb of pain.
I look beyond, where purer joys
  Delight my longing eyes;
And so I thank Him from my heart
  For what His love denies.

How tenderly He leadeth me
  When earthly hopes are dim;
And when I falter by the way,
  He bids me lean on Him.
He lifts my soul above the clouds
  Where friendship never dies;
And so I thank Him from my heart
  For what His love denies.

Fanny Crosby
Jan. 6/99

Ed. The manuscript carries several notations, including the initials "M.S." and the name
"H. P. Main." There is also the question "Is this O.K.?" signed by "I.A.S."—Ira Allan
Sankey—and the further notes "O.K." and "This is fine." At upper right the paper is
embossed with the name "HAMILTON."

5165

Able to Deliver Thee

If thy faith can say that the Lord is thine,
  O believing heart, will thou yet repine?
If thy hope is built on His word divine,
  Let thy care on Him be cast.

Chorus: He is able still to deliver thee,
            And His own right [hand] thy defense shall be;
            He is able still to deliver thee,
            And to bring thee home at last.

He has borne the cross and His life He gave,
  He has conquered death and has rent the grave,
He redeemed the world and is strong to save—
  Let thy care on Him be cast.
                Chorus.

O resign thy all to His holy will,
  For He saves (thee) now and will save (thee) still;
And thy soul with joy let His promise fill;
  Thou shalt overcome at last.
                Chorus.

Fanny Crosby
Feb. 3/99

Ed.   In the final stanza, the word "thee" appears twice as "the." In the chorus the word "hand" seems to be required.

95

5174

I Will Bless Thee

Thou did'st love me, O my Savior,
  When my heart was far from Thee;
Thou did'st give Thyself a ransom
  To atone for one like me.

Chorus: I will praise Thee, I will bless Thee,
    For the peace Thy love bestows,
    And the fountain Thou hast opened,
    That to all so freely flows.

I will praise Thee, O my Savior,
  For the message I have heard,
And the lessons Thou hast taught me
  By the Spirit—through Thy word.
              Chorus.

I will praise Thee, O my Savior,
  For Thy tender, patient care,
And the promise that assures me
  Thou wilt hear and answer prayer.
              Chorus.

Fanny Crosby
Feb. 28/99

Ed.   Across the scrap of heavy paper (7¾" × 4¾"), someone has blue-penciled "written to
I.A.S." At the bottom, in the same handwriting, is "Dec. 02."

5184

The Greatest of All Is Love

When faith shall close her radiant eyes,
   And hope in full fruition dies,
Immortal love beyond the skies
   Will fill the realms above.

Chorus: Though faith is our victory through Christ our King,
           And great are the blessings from hope that spring,
           Yet, filled with the fulness of joy, we sing
           "The greatest of these is love."

Love suffers long and thinks no ill,
   Seeks not her own, but others' weal;
The broken heart—'tis hers to heal,
   With balm from heaven above.
              Chorus.

Love hopes, endures, believes all things;
   Love soars aloft on timeless wings.
In sorrow's night of gloom she brings
   Glad echoes from above.
              Chorus.

Fanny Crosby
Mar. 14/99

Ed. The above version of the chorus has been added on a separate piece of paper and pinned
    to the poem. The original refrain was:
       Love shineth forever, a constant flame,
         Eternity's ages shall bless her name,
       And numbers unnumbered in song proclaim—
         "The greatest of these is love."
    The poem appears on a piece of Biglow & Main note paper that carries the notice:
    "Agents for Curwen's Tonic Sol-fa Publications."

5195

Rejoice!

Rejoice, rejoice, O pilgrim!
  Lift up thine eyes and see,
Beyond the mists and shadows,
  The light that shines for thee.
'Tis God's own light of promise,
  His smile of perfect peace;
And soon, with Him forever,
  Thy weary march shall cease.

Rejoice, rejoice, O pilgrim!
  And hail the blessed light,
Whose tranquil beams are leading
  Beyond this vale of night.
Let love, thy soul inspiring,
  Thy faith and hope increase;
Till, safe among the ransomed,
  Thy weary march shall cease.

Rejoice, rejoice, O pilgrim!
  The Master's work fulfill.
The light that cheers thy pathway
  Is shining brighter still.
Press onward, O press onward
  To realms of perfect peace,
Where, in the Father's kingdom,
  Thy weary march shall cease.

Fanny Crosby
Mar. 23/99

5196

We Belong to Jesus

Not our own, no, not our own,
   We belong to Jesus.
Saved by grace through faith alone,
   We belong to Jesus.

Chorus: On the cross for you and me,
           On the cross of Calvary,
           Since He died to make us free,
           We belong to Jesus.

For the blood that freely flows,
   Glory be to Jesus!
For the joy His love bestows,
   Glory be to Jesus!
                  Chorus.

He from sin our ransom paid,
   Praise the name of Jesus!
Full atonement He has made,
   Praise the name of Jesus!
                  Chorus.

Fanny Crosby
Mar. 23/99

99

5197

The Lord Is Our Hope

The Lord is our hope and salvation,
  His word is our counsel and guide;
The Lord is our strength and Redeemer,
  The rock where in safety we hide.

Chorus: He dwells in the hearts of His people,
      And holdeth their lives in His hands;
      His mercy endureth forever
      To such as obey His commands.

The Lord is a refuge in trouble,
  Our shelter where'er we may be;
He speaks, and the tempest is silent,
  He ruleth the waves of the sea.
          Chorus.

The Lord is a gracious defender,
  His truth is more precious than gold;
His love like a banner is o'er us,
  His glory and grace we behold.
          Chorus.

Fanny Crosby
Mar. 23/99

5214

His Hands and His Side

Away on the cold, barren mountains,
   Alone (in) the tempter's control,
I knew not the love I was slighting,
   Till Jesus spoke peace to my soul.

Chorus: He came, and His words were so tender,
      They humbled my spirit of pride;
      And then, with a look of compassion,
      He showed me His hands and His side.

Away on the cold, barren mountains
   I wandered in sin and despair;
My hope had gone out in the darkness,
   Till Jesus came seeking me there.
            Chorus.

And now, while I tell the glad story
   Of love and redemption so free,
O wonder of wonders the greatest—
   That Jesus had pity on me.
            Chorus.

Fanny Crosby
Apr. 21/99

Ed.   These lines were written in ink on unlined, quality paper, about 7″ x 9½″. The second
line appears "Alone at the tempter's control" on the original manuscript. The page also
bears a Biglow & Main stamp with the same date given above.

101

5244

That Land of Song

There is a friend, a precious friend,
    Whose all-protecting power
Can wreathe in smiles the darkest cloud,
    In sorrow's dreary hour.

Chorus: O blessed place, by Him prepared,
        Where dwell a blissful throng,
        Whose golden harps with rapture fill
        That land of love and song.

There is a friend, a precious friend,
    Who knows our every care;
And they who overcome by faith
    A victor crown may wear.
                Chorus.

That precious friend is Christ the Lord—
    Hosanna to His name!
That we may join His ransomed ones,
    And swell their loud acclaim.
                Chorus.

Fanny Crosby
May 26/99

Ed.   The original was written on heavy note paper 4½" x 6⅞".

God of Eternity

God of eternity, Savior and King!
  Help us to honor Thee, help while we sing;
Now may the clouds of night
  Break into splendor bright,
Jesus, our life and light,
  Our Lord and King!

God of eternity, Ancient of Days,
  Glorious in majesty, author of praise;
Hear Thou our earnest call,
  While at Thy feet we fall,
Jesus, our all in all,
  Our Lord and King!

God of eternity, Thee we proclaim!
  God of the earth and sea, love is Thy name;
Lord, through Thine only Son,
  Thy work of grace hath done;
O blessed Three in One,
  Thy name we sing!

Ed. This manuscript was difficult to decipher because of its many corrections. The last line
of stanzas one and two was first "Jesus our King," then "O Savior King" and finally "Our
Lord and King." It was signed "Fanny Crosby, Jan. 19, 1900" and bore the number
"5306," but these notations were crossed out, as if the poem was not to be credited to
her.

103

5342

Only Believe

Come to the fountain of mercy
  Jesus has opened for thee;
Cleansed in its pure flowing waters,
  Whiter than snow thou shalt be.

Chorus: Now the Redeemer is waiting,
          Waiting thy soul to reclaim;
          He will receive and forgive thee,
          Only believe on His name.

Heed not the voice of the tempter,
  Leave the dark mountains of sin;
Knock at the door of salvation,
  Jesus will bid thee come in.
                Chorus.

Haste to the Savior that loves thee,
  He is thy refuge and rest;
Haste to the arms that will fold thee
  Gently and safe on His breast.
                Chorus.

Thursday evening
Mar. 7, 1901

Ed.   At the bottom of the original is penciled "Fanny Crosby?"

5373

In the Shadow of the Highest

When the toils of life are many,
　　And our hearts are worn with care,
When we faint beneath the burden
　　Of a cross we cannot bear;

Chorus:　In the shadow of the Highest,
　　　　In His secret place of rest—
　　　　O the welcome that awaits us
　　　　Where His chosen ones are blest.

In the shadow of the Highest,
　　What a vision of delight!
Floods of joy from golden regions
　　Burst with rapture on our sight.
　　　　　　　　Chorus.

In the shadow of the Highest,
　　Like a dream the moments glide;
And we learn the songs of Eden,
　　While in peace we there abide.
　　　　　　　　Chorus.

Fanny Crosby

October 23, 1902

"He that dwelleth in the secret place of the Most High shall abide
under the shadow of the Almighty." 　　　　　Psalm XCI, 1.

105

5384

He Died for You, He Died for Me

O Love divine, amazing Love,
   That brought to earth from heaven above
The Son of God for us to die,
   That we might dwell with Him on high.

Chorus: He died for you, He died for me,
      And shed His blood to make us free;
      Upon the cross of Calvary
      The Savior died for you and me.

For us the crown of thorns He bore,
   For us the robe of scorn He wore;
He conquered death and rent the grave,
   And lives again our souls to save.
         Chorus.

O wanderer, come, on Him believe,
   His offered grace by faith receive;
Awake, arise, and hear Him call,
   The feast is spread—there's room for all.
         Chorus.

Fanny Crosby

Feb. 11, 1903
Phila., Pa.

Ed.   The original was penned on a heavy bit of paper about 5″ x 7½″ in size.

5388

Thou Art with Me

Thou art with me, blessed Savior,
　　Every moment, every hour;
I adore Thee for Thy mercy,
　　And Thy wondrous keeping power.

Chorus:　O'er my life, Thy love presiding,
　　　　　Step by step, my way is guiding;
　　　　　In the Rock my soul is hiding—
　　　　　"Rock of ages, cleft for me."

I am resting on Thy promise,
　　I am trusting only Thee;
And rejoicing in the fullness
　　Of Thy grace that makes me free.
　　　　　　　　　　Chorus.

Thou hast led me, O my Savior,
　　And Thy hand will lead me still;
Through the valley and the shadow
　　I shall walk, and fear no ill.
　　　　　　　　　　Chorus.

Fanny Crosby
Jan. 28, 1903

Ed.　The poem appears on heavy note paper 5″ x 7¾″.

107

Welcome Home

Welcome hour, from labor free,
  When our souls at peace may be,
And in sweet communion blend
  With our firm-abiding Friend.

Chorus: Gracious God, Eternal Lord,
        Thou in earth and heaven adored,
        Thou to whom archangels bow—
        Come and bless Thy people now.

Through the cares and ills of life,
  Through its toils and weary strife,
By Thy hand, from day to day,
  Thou hast led us all the way.
              Chorus.

May our hearts, with strong desire,
  More and more to Thee aspire;
Upward drawn by faith and love,
  To a home prepared above.
              Chorus.

Fanny Crosby
Perth Amboy
N.J.

April 28, 1903

Ed. We may guess that the transcriber made an error in the title, since the emphasis of the
hymn is on "an hour" of worship or fellowship with God. It probably should be
"Welcome Hour." The words appear on personal light green note paper, 4½" x 6¾".

108

5396

Our Deliverer

The Lord is our deliverer
  When doubts and fears arise;
We see the bow of promise
  That shines amid the skies.

Chorus: His love, our shield and banner,
       Is o'er us night and day;
       He takes from us our burdens,
       And rolls the clouds away.

The Lord is our deliverer,
  The Rock in whom we trust;
Our strength and our Redeemer,
  The only wise and just.
              Chorus.

The Lord is our deliverer,
  O praise His Holy Name!
The bliss of life eternal
  Through Him our souls may claim.
              Chorus.

Geneva, N.Y.
May 21st, 1903
Fanny Crosby

Ed.   These words were written with fine penmanship on a heavy piece of paper 5¼″ x 6⅝″, carrying the incomplete watermark "French ..." The back of the sheet bears the rubber-stamped date "May 23, 1903."

109

5399

Peace Be Thine

May 30th, 1903

Peace, peace be thine,
O trembling soul.
Come, and the Savior
Will make thee whole.
Far, far from home,
Why longer stray?
Come, and believing,
His voice obey.

Rest, rest in Him,
Thy gracious Lord.
Hope in His mercy,
And trust His word.
Rest, rest in Him,
From sorrow free;
Love like a fountain
Still flows for thee.

Fanny Crosby

Ed. The two stanzas appear on the personal stationery of Henry Cobham, Gladerun, Pa.,
with the additional address "Stonylonesome"—probably the home name. The Cobham
family crest appears in the upper left and includes the motto "Animus est nobilitas."
The paper bears the watermark "Superior Mills."

5402

Peace Be Thine

Peace be thine, child of sorrow,
   Watch and wait—a blessed morrow,
Full of gladness, free from sadness,
   Now in glory dawns for thee.
Look, behold! the light is coming,
   One by one the shadows fly;
Hope again returns to cheer thee,
   Clouds no longer veil the sky.

Chorus: Peace be thine, the night is waning,
      Thou a song of praise will sing;
      Grief may bide a guest at evening,
      But the morrow joy will bring.

Peace be thine, cease thy weeping;
   Trust in Him who, never sleeping,
Goes before thee, watches o'er thee,
   Through His Spirit all thy days.
Trust in Him, whose love so tender,
   Lays thy head upon His breast;
And, amid thy deepest trial,
   Lulls thy breaking heart to rest.
          Chorus.

Peace be thine, still abounding;
   Peace be thine, thy path surrounding,
Like a river, flowing ever,
   From the pearly gates above.
Haste thee on without a murmur,
   Lo! the end is drawing nigh;
Haste thee on, O weary traveler,
   To a palace built on high.
          Chorus.

Fanny Crosby
Warren, Pa.
June 9, 1903

Ed. Fanny Crosby wrote two poems with this title, evidently ten days apart, while visiting at the Henry Cobham home in Pennsylvania. (See the previous page.) This one is on the back of another piece of personal Cobham stationery, with the address "Warren, Pa."

Into the Sunshine

Come out into the sunshine
  That sparkles ever bright;
Why should we walk in darkness
  When Jesus is the light?
'Tis He, who now before us,
  Unveils the golden rays,
That change the night of mourning
  To songs of joy and praise.

Chorus: O welcome now the sunshine,
       While music through the air
       Is borne aloft on seraph wings
       To yonder clime so fair.
       O welcome now its glory
       That sparkles ever bright,
       We do not walk in darkness,
       For Jesus is the light.

Come out into the sunshine,
  Where pleasant pastures grow,
And let us walk together
  By cooling streams that flow;
Among the hills and valleys
  The harp of nature rings,
And all the vast creation
  Adore the King of Kings.
                    Chorus.

Come out into the sunshine,
  And happy let us be,
To know its beams of gladness
  To every one are free;
O, dwell amid the sunshine
  Of pure and holy love;
The gift of our Creator,
  Who brought it from above.
                    Chorus.

                              Fanny J. Crosby
           Warren, Pa.   June 11, 1903

Ed.   This poem was typed on a 6″ x 10¼″ sheet with an incomplete watermark "Brookd. .e
Linen Bond." The name, address and date are in pencil.

5404

The Lord Will be a Light Unto Me

I know that my God will hear me,
  And answer whene'er I call,
I know that His power will keep me,
  Nor suffer my feet to fall.

Chorus:　I know that my God will hear me;
　　　　I'll trust in His grace so free,
　　　　And when I sit in the darkness,
　　　　The Lord will be light unto me.

I know that my God will hear me;
  His promise He cannot break,
I know He will guard me safely,
  And never His child forsake.
　　　　　　Chorus.

I know that my God will hear me;
  I know He will grant my prayer.
For still, on my heart reflected,
  His image of love I bear.
　　　　　　Chorus.

O light of my Father's glory,
  Its luster will ne'er decay,
But still in my soul abiding,
  'Twill shine to the perfect day.
　　　　　　Chorus.

                                    Fanny Crosby
            Williamsport, Pa.　June 16, 1903

Hugh, at first I had this for last verse. You can take which is liked
best, or you need not have but three verses.

O Light of eternal glory,
  That fills me again with song,
And wakens with pure devotion
  The chords that have slumbered long.
  (or, My harp that has slumbered long.)

Ed.　The note at the bottom is obviously a message from Fanny Crosby to Hubert P. Main.
The back of the page gives the acknowledgment "Rec'd Jun 18 1903." The paper
watermark has a crown, and underneath "Hurlbut's Court of England."

113

5407

At the Cross

At the cross I was kneeling,
   When the Lord, Himself revealing,
Gave me peace in believing,
   When I sought His mercy there.

In the cross I will glory,
   And to all proclaim the story
How I found my Redeemer,
   And He heard my humble prayer.

To the cross I am clinging,
   And my faith and hope are singing
Songs of praise to my Savior,
   For His kind and gentle care.

I was lost but He found me,
   With His love divine He bound me;
O, my full heart adores Him,
   For He heard my humble prayer.

Fanny Crosby
Phila., Pa.   June 24th, 1903

Ed.   At the top of the sheet the date June 26, 1903 is rubber-stamped, and the notation appears "Music by I. A. (Allan) Sankey"—indicating the son of D. L. Moody's associate, Ira D. Sankey.

There Is One

2.

There is One, that like a shepherd will defend our way,
   And He looks with eyes of pity on the sheep that stray;
From the mountains wild and lonely, still He calls them to His
   fold,
   He is full of grace and mercy—His love can ne'er be told.
         Chorus.

3.

There is One, that like a shepherd will defend our way,
   We shall see, adore and praise Him thro' a long, bright day;
In the kingdom of the faithful we shall lay our armor down,
   And from Him, our Lord and Savior, receive a starry crown.
         Chorus.

Fanny J. Crosby
Dec. 26, 30, 1902; Jany. (sic) 7, 1903

Ed.   Obviously the first stanza and chorus of this song are missing; what remains is written on
the back of a Biglow & Main letterhead with the address "135 Fifth Avenue, New York,
N.Y."; the company moved there in the early 20th century. Part of the watermark
appears: "xtra strong."
A heavy blue pencil (evidently used by I. Allan Sankey) has underlined the first three
words, indicating the song's title, and also added the words "Written to I.A.S., Dec.
24, 02." It is surmised that Mr. Sankey gave the melody to Fanny Crosby on that date.
She may have had difficulty with the unusual meter—13.13.15.14—since she evidently
worked on the poem over a period of two weeks.

Our Rally Song

Another bright vacation,
   A restful, calm repose,
Another golden summer
   Has reached its golden close.
Renewed in health and vigor,
   And filled with love and praise,
We bless the gracious Giver,
   Whose goodness crowns our days.

Behold there comes a message
   In tones that speak to all:
"Return to active labor,
   Obey the Savior's call,
Go sound the gospel trumpet,
   Proclaim redemption free,
Go rescue those who perish
   Wherever they may be."

O rally for the Master,
   And may the Spirit's power
Inspire with true devotion
   This consecrated hour.
In Him, our King eternal,
   May every soul rejoice,
And shout aloud His glory
   In one united voice.

Rally, youthful soldiers!
   Rally round the cross!
Wave the royal standard,
   Count the world but dross.
Swell the joyful chorus,
   March with sword and shield,
Follow our Commander,
   Onward to the field.

Chorus: Rally, then, you soldiers,
      Rally round the cross!
      Wave the royal standard,
      Count all else but loss.

Fanny J. Crosby
September 1911
Copyright, 1911 by the Biglow-Main Co.

Ed.   The fourth "stanza" is in a different meter than the previous three, and is obviously part
of a long chorus; to corroborate this, there is a line of dashes following the third stanza.
The reverse side of the typed copy bears a Biglow and Main stamp used to record the
amount of "stamps, coins and bills" enclosed with orders. It is dated Oct. 4, 1911. The
paper's watermark appears to be "Guinnipiack Mills."

I'll Praise My Redeemer

I'll praise my Redeemer as long as I live,
  His name my rejoicing shall be;
All honor and glory to Him will I give
  For what He accomplished for me.

Chorus: His banner of mercy is over my head,
      The cloud and the pillar I see;
      I'll praise my Redeemer and hallow His name
      For all His compassion to me.

I'll praise my Redeemer, the light of my soul,
  Who graciously heareth my call.
I'll praise Him, though billows like mountains may roll,
  For He is my refuge, my all.
            Chorus.

I'll praise my Redeemer, my Savior and King,
  My precious Defender and Lord.
Forever and ever of Him would I sing,
  And rest on the arm of His word.
            Chorus.

And when He shall call me from earth to depart,
  And soar to the arms of His love,
I'll praise my Redeemer, the strength of my heart,
  With all His dear children above.
            Chorus.

Ed. On the reverse side of the page, this is penciled: "Fanny J. Crosby. Pd. . . . (name not
     decipherable, possibly 'Mrs. Sankey') 3/20/16."
     The paper's watermark is "Old Berkshire Mills, 1888."

117

Thursday Sep. 14th   *Fanny Crosby*

    For the joys of full salvation
        And the peace those joys afford:
    Let our souls, and all within us,
        Magnify and praise the Lord.

    Chorus: Praise Him, all ye floods of ocean;
              Praise Him, all ye stars above;
              Praise Him, every living creature;
              Praise and sing His wondrous love.

We were lost till Jesus found us,
    Till His blood our ransom paid;
Now the gate of life is open,
    Full atonement He has made.
                    Chorus.

Sound aloud the gospel trumpet,
    Shout aloud the sweet refrain:
Blessed be the Lord forever,
    Blessed be His holy name.
                    Chorus.

Ed.   The manuscript has the "CONGRESS" seal embossed at upper left, and the name
"Fanny Crosby" is in quite a different script from the rest of the page. At the bottom,
someone has penciled "no date."

Thy Promise

O bless the hour we set apart
   And consecrate for fervent prayer;
Thou knowest every longing heart,
   And every throb of care.

Chorus: O, may Thy spirit from above
          Now rest upon us like a dove;
          To purest thoughts each heart inspire,
          And light within the sacred fire.

Behold Thy children, gracious Lord,
   Whose prayer, ascending to the skies,
Would claim the promise of Thy word
   For this, our humble sacrifice.
             Chorus.

Our soul's request Thou dost fulfill,
   Our faith looks up with placid brow;
And, leaning on Thy promise still,
   Believe our prayer is answered now.
             Chorus.

Words by *Fanny Crosby*

Ed.   The original is one of the few typewritten pages, but it has no punctuation. It was
probably typed as it was dictated by Fanny Crosby.

119

Lo! the smiling earth rejoices,
  Come, come away.
Let us tune our hearts and voices,
  Join, join the lay.
We'll sing our great Creator's praise,
  How just and true are all His ways;
His tender mercy crowns our days,
  His love is free to all.

Chorus: Come to the fountain,
          The fountain of life that flows;
          Come to the fountain
          That flows free for all.

King of glory, we adore Thee;
  Hail, Prince of peace!
Angels cast their crowns before Thee,
  Hail, Prince of peace!
To Him, the Lamb for sinners slain,
  To Him, who died and lives again,
Let music breathe her sweetest strain
  For love so free to all.
                              Chorus.

Still our youthful footsteps guiding,
  Kind, kind is He.
Still for every want providing,
  Kind, kind is He.
He gives His children sweet repose,
  Their every pain He feels and knows,
While every heart with rapture glows
  For love so free to all.
                              Chorus.

                                    Fanny

Ed.   This was found in a handwriting that rarely appears in the manuscripts and the copy is
      almost illegible because of water-spotting, etc. These words are penciled across the top:
      "I doubt about using this. There is not much point to it."

Only a Moment

Only a moment, my Savior, with Thee,
　Only a moment in secret for prayer,
Only the light of Thy presence to see,
　Then I am ready my burden to bear.

(Repeat first four lines for chorus)

Restful and happy, a child of Thy love,
　What are the trials that compass me here?
Soon shall I enter the mansions above,
　Nothing to grieve me, and nothing to fear.
Chorus.

Only a moment of blessing divine,
　Gently refreshing my soul like the dew,
Only a whisper to tell I am Thine,
　Then will I gladly my life-work renew.
Chorus.

Toiling wherever my duty may call,
　Climbing the mountain, though rugged and steep,
Praising Thy goodness and trusting for all,
　Knowing in safety my way Thou wilt keep.
Chorus.

Only a moment to sit at Thy feet,
　Only a foretaste of what I shall be,
When with the ransomed in glory I meet,
　Clothed and made perfect, O Savior, in Thee.
Chorus.

Only a moment to watch and to wait,
　Biding my time till my summons I hear,
Then shall I enter the beautiful gate,
　Nothing to grieve me, and nothing to fear.
Chorus.

Words by *Fanny Crosby*

Ed.　The original copy was typed, using a blue and red ribbon; the title and "chorus" indication are in red. An incomplete watermark appears to be "Brother Jonathan Bond."

INDEX

The basic listing is of first lines;
separate titles are in italics.